CYNTHIA HICKEY

COOKING WITH LOVE

Finding Love the Harvey Girl Way
Book 1

Cynthia Hickey

Copyright © **2015**
Written by: Cynthia Hickey
Published by: Winged Publications
Cover Design: Cynthia Hickey

This book is a work of fiction. Names, characters, places, and incidents are the product of the author's imagination and are used fictitiously. Any resemblance to actual events, locales, or persons, living or dead, is coincidental.

No part of this book may be copied or distributed without the author's consent.

All rights reserved.

ISBN: 1512262927
ISBN-13: 9781512262926

DEDICATION

As always, to my husband, Tom, and to God. Both who never give up on me..

Trust in the Lord and do good; dwell in the land and enjoy safe pasture. Take delight in the Lord, and he will give you the desires of your heart. Commit your way to the Lord; trust in him and he will do this..

-Psalms 37:3-5

COOKING WITH LOVE

1

1876 St. Louis, Missouri

Tabitha McClelland twisted her apron, the fabric so soiled she believed it could stand up on its own. She straightened her shoulders as the first train of the day screeched to a halt, and wished for something nicer to wear. The least her new employer could do was to give her something clean on her first day. Obviously, a previous employee left in a hurry and no one thought to do laundry.

Taking a deep breath, she stepped forward to open the door. Her heart leaped into her throat. Black smoke belched from the engine and drifted inside the dining room, mixing with the odor of burned bacon and sour grease. Within minutes a crowd of passengers surged inside.

On the first morning at her new job, she'd expected

more than the dirty eatery with a scuffed wooden floor and the soiled aprons she and the other woman wore over their equally stained gray uniforms. She needed to look past the filth and muddle through because she sorely needed the work. Aprons could be washed.

"Step aside, Tabby," Alice, her coworker barked. Sweat stained the bodice of her blouse. Dark hair streaked with silver escaped from her bun. "Seat the customers, then join me in the kitchen."

Tabby dashed among the passengers handing out tattered menus printed on newsprint before she rushed to join Alice. "Now what?" Tabby glanced at the plates of runny eggs and greasy beans that lined the counter. Her stomach churned.

"We wait until it's almost time for the customers to board. Then we serve them."

"What about taking their orders?"

The waitress laughed. "Those are just for show. The only difference is what the person wants to drink. Relax."

"But, the food's waiting and growing cold." Not to mention getting more unappetizing by the minute. As the words left her lips, Tabby wanted them back. She knew better than to question her superiors, but her mouth ran like a racehorse most of the time, crashing over the line at the end without warning.

"Hush, girl. You don't want Mr. Beeker to hear you asking questions." Alice frowned and lowered her voice. "If you value your job, you'll be quiet and do as you're told."

Tabby eyed the pudgy, balding man reading a newspaper in the corner. Her flesh crawled at remembrance of the leer on his face when he'd granted her the waitress job. She shuddered. Other than picking up her pay, she hoped her interview with Mr. Beeker would be all the contact she had with the man. Since the age of sixteen, Tabby had made do on her own. She didn't need a man to take care of her. Especially one old enough to be her grandpa.

Voices rose from the dining room. Tabby glanced at the clock. The train would leave in ten minutes. Mr. Beeker strolled past, the newspaper folded under his arm.

"Go collect their money," Alice said.

Tabby scrambled to do her bidding. Why were they taking the money before serving the food? Was that right? What kind of business had she gotten herself into here?

"Miss?" A gentleman in a suit raised his hand as she finished the task. "Will we be eating soon? The train will be leaving shortly."

"Yeah! And why do we have to pay before we get our food?" A bearded man scowled.

Tabby swallowed past the lump in her throat and tried to smile, failing miserably. "I'll check on that right now, sir." She pocketed the fistful of half-dollars and rushed back to Alice. "The customers are asking about their food."

Alice glanced at the clock. "We can serve now. Make it snappy. We've got to get a plate in front of each customer before the whistle blows."

Tabby bit the inside of her lip. She might not be experienced in such matters, but it seemed as if they were doing things backward. She'd no sooner set the last plate in front of an elderly woman when the train's whistle blew. Pandemonium broke out as the people shoved back chairs, grabbed children's hands, and bustled outside. All without eating a bite. One man scurried back, grabbed a piece of toast from his plate, and nodded before following the others.

"Help me clear the tables, then set the plates back on the counter for the next crowd," Alice said as she began collecting plates. "And, replace that piece of toast."

Tabby planted her fists on her hips. "Are we reusing the food?" Unbelievable. "This is unethical! We take the people's money and serve the food too late for them to eat. People do this every day?"

"Hush. Mr. Beeker will hear you. The walls aren't that thick in here." Alice pushed past her. "It's the way things are done."

"It's wrong." Tabby glanced out the window. A girl in pigtails looked over her shoulder before stepping on board. "Those people left here hungry."

"And unless they packed a lunch, they'll most likely be hungry at the next stop, too. Railroad diners have to make a living too, you know. There aren't many job opportunities out there for women, so hush." Alice slammed the plates down. Her lined face reddened. "We get enough bad attention being waitresses without frequenting less respectable places. A girl has to make do where she can. If you don't like it, you can move on. There'll be somebody to take your place soon enough."

Tabby pulled the money from her pocket, counted out a day's pay, and then handed the rest to Alice. "I quit."

"Wait a minute!" Mr. Beeker reentered the room. "There'll be another train in an hour."

"I apologize for inconveniencing you." Tabby untied her apron and let it drop to the floor. Jutting her chin, she marched to the changing room and donned her navy skirt and white shirtwaist, ignoring Mr. Beeker's heated words.

Unemployed again, but she had a few coins in her pocket. She'd manage somehow. With a skip in her step, she hurried outside. Spring sunshine and a gentle breeze caressed her face, reminding her the day was too lovely to be spent inside a dark dining room anyway.

Buggies lined the road and passengers crowded the sidewalk awaiting the arrival of the next train. Tabby wanted to warn them to box food to take along. If she ever got the opportunity to ride a train west, she'd never be caught off guard like those poor souls who left the station as hungry as when they arrived. A girl was wise to keep her wits about her. She stepped off the sidewalk and dodged people and horses until she reached Main Street.

A wooden bench beckoned from beneath a towering oak tree. Tabby accepted its invitation and sat, trying desperately to ignore her rumbling stomach. From unemployed to employed and back to unemployed in a matter of a couple hours. Sighing, she slumped forward and rested her elbows on her knees. With no time for the luxury of looking for new employment, and no more than a few coins in her pocket, she would have to take the first thing to come along. Her gaze traveled the street, searching for a potential place to apply.

A little help here, God. She snorted. Like He'd been much help in the past. Still, it never hurt to ask.

She could go back to being somebody's maid or nanny, but only as a last resort. It was not that she didn't like children, she did, but Tabby wanted adventure. She wanted to meet new people! Maybe she could get a teaching certificate. Move on to a new place after a year.

A newspaper lodged under the bush beside the bench caught her attention. Tabby bent and retrieved it, flipping idly through the pages. Maybe there would be an advertisement for a job. Her breath caught as her gaze landed on bold black letters.

WANTED:

Young women, eighteen to thirty years of age, of good moral character, attractive and intelligent as waitresses in Harvey Eating Houses on the Santa Fe Railroad in the West. Wages $17.50 per month with room and board. Liberal tips customary. Experience not necessary. Write Fred Harvey, Union Depot, Kansas City, Missouri.

~

There was! And it paid more than the job she'd quit. A salary and tips. Bouncing on the bench, she bit back a shriek. The ad was an answer to her prayer. Here was something she could do and have a chance to see the West. She folded the paper and leaped to her feet. She had a few sheets of writing paper and at least one envelope at the boarding house. She'd write and apply today.

~

After days of eating one meal a day to spread out what little money she had, and checking the mail obsessively, Tabby's patience had paid off. She squirmed in the church pew. Finally, life was taking an exciting turn. Tomorrow, she would catch a train to Chicago for her interview.

"Ladies of St. Louis."

Tabby jerked, her attention riveted back on the

reverend. She might not attend church every Sunday, but doing so before starting a new life couldn't hurt.

The pastor peered over his specs at the congregation, a severe lift to his eyebrows. "I'm sure many of you have seen the papers and the scandalous advertisement by a Mr. Fred Harvey. Shameless."

Surely, the people of the church didn't condemn her choice of a new job?

"This man has come up with a crazy scheme to lure innocent young women into the debauchery of the Wild West. Reputations will be ruined. Bordellos will be over-run with our daughters as they're left to fend for themselves and paraded in front of leering men like cattle at auction."

Around Tabby, women cried into handkerchiefs and men tightened their lips in disapproval. The pastor had to be wrong. Wasn't he? Waitressing was an honorable profession, correct? She didn't want to be stranded in a strange land and branded as a loose woman, but a girl needed to earn a paycheck.

Maybe it was the fact that young girls were leaving home and striking out on their own that had folks in a dither. But, young women like Tabby didn't have a family to care for them.

She grasped her pocketbook and slipped out of the pew. Her spirit sagged around her knees as she left the church and stepped into the cloud of humidity blanketing the town. How could people think waitressing was a bad profession for women? Or was it more the location of the restaurants along the railroad that had folks in a tizzy?

She passed a diner. The aroma of roasting meat drifted through the open door. Her mouth watered, and her stomach rumbled. What she wouldn't give for a big plate of roast beef, gravy, and mashed potatoes. Weeks, maybe months, had passed since she'd felt really full after a meal. Her thoughts returned to the pastor's words.

She had no choice but to go to the interview. She'd already received her ticket. Chicago was a bustling city. If the interview seemed strange or made her uncomfortable, she'd find another job. There was nothing for her here. Time to bid St. Louis adieu.

~

Adam Foster noticed the pretty woman before she sat down across the aisle from him. Blonde hair tucked neatly into a bun, chocolate brown eyes that flitted back and forth in search of a place to sit. He was glad there was one girl too sensible to succumb to the ridiculous fashion of wearing a bustle and excessive ruffles. Her simple navy suit complemented her tiny frame and didn't impose on anyone else's space.

She plopped onto the seat with a sigh and gazed out the window, a winsome expression on her face. Had she left family or a beau behind? Adam shrugged and transferred his attention back to his newspaper. It wasn't any of his business, even if he did enjoy wondering where other folks were headed.

He needed to focus on getting to Chicago to find out the location of his new job as head chef in one of Fred Harvey's restaurants. When Mr. Harvey had strolled into the place Adam previously worked and tasted his food, the man wasted no time offering him a job. Adam would own his own place in no time with the hefty salary Harvey was paying. The future looked brighter than it had in a long time.

A man with slicked back hair and a leer on his face approached the lovely girl. "May I sit here?" He lowered himself into the seat.

She looked up and frowned. Her face paled. "This seat is taken."

"Doesn't look as if anyone is sitting here to me." He leaned closer to her.

"You take liberties, sir." She pressed into the seat. "There are plenty of empty seats on the train."

Apparently, the young lady didn't welcome the man's attention. Adam stood and moved past him. "Sorry, sir. This is my seat. Hello, darling. Sorry I'm late." He smiled at his new companion and hoped she'd pick up his cue and play along.

"Oh." Her eyes widened, then narrowed. "What took you so long?"

"Making sure our bags are secure." He clapped the man on the shoulder and winked. "They are. Couldn't wait to get back."

The stranger tipped his hat and stood. "My apologies." He strode down the aisle and plopped next to another young woman.

Adam turned to the red-faced young lady. "Sorry, but you looked like you needed rescuing."

She lifted her chin and glared. "I didn't unless it was to breathe, but thank you all the same. His cologne would've choked a horse. You may return to your seat now."

Adam laughed, eliciting a reluctant smile from her. For a moment he thought he'd receive a slap for his troubles. He sat beside her. "I'm Adam Foster, and I would enjoy the company, if you don't mind. I'd like to think if my younger sister were traveling alone, a kind man would come to her aid if needed."

"Tabitha McClelland. Friends call me Tabby." Her eyes twinkled. "Since you seem to have no intention of changing seats, , I guess that gives you the right to call me Tabby."

"Guess so. Where're you headed?"

"Chicago. I have a job interview with a Mr. Fred Harvey."

"So, you'll be one of Harvey's girls."

She stiffened. "Is that bad? Do I *want* to be one of his girls? I'm not sure I like that title."

He chuckled. "You'll be fine. I work for Mr. Harvey. I'm a chef, and I can guarantee there isn't anything immoral about working for him. Besides, you'll interview with his wife."

She sighed. "That's a relief, especially since I'll be a waitress in one of his restaurants." She scooted to face him. "Is he a good man?"

"From what I've heard, he expects a lot from his employees but is a fair man." Adam patted her gloved hand. "Don't worry." Not having actually spent a lot of time in Harvey's company, other than the rare demonstrations of the man's temper, which he didn't feel he needed to tell Tabby about, Adam hadn't heard anything alarming. "You'll be surrounded by plenty of other women and properly chaperoned."

"Wonderful." She dug in her faded carpetbag and pulled out a sandwich wrapped in oiled paper. After a moment, she held it up to him. "Would you like to share?"

In the second she'd had her bag open, Adam could see there wasn't another one. He wouldn't be a gentleman if he took even half of her only sandwich.

"No, thank you. If you get the job with Harvey, you won't need to take your lunch to your final destination. All his employees eat free."

She shuddered. "I couldn't. I've seen what railroad diners serve."

"Yet you've applied for a job in one? You've seen nothing like a Harvey restaurant. I promise you'll be surprised and pleased." Adam shifted to find a more comfortable position for his long legs. "You'll bunk in a Pullman car if the ride extends overnight. Only the finest for Harvey's employees."

"Then I hope I'm hired." She bit into her sandwich. "Are you sure you don't want anything? I have an apple."

"Positive, but thank you." Her sweet, trusting demeanor reminded him too much of Marilyn. Two years since his wife's death, and he still hadn't reconciled himself to the title of widower. He transferred his attention out the window. Maybe the Harvey rules of male employees not keeping company with the female ones were for the best. He wouldn't be encouraged to pursue a relationship that might leave him with another broken heart.

The train rolled past fields of hay, and as evening fell, Adam wished he'd decided to go to Chicago earlier in the day so he could've stretched out in one of the Pullman cars he'd bragged about to Tabby. By the time he bought his ticket, they'd all been full. He'd be as stiff as a corpse come morning. He cut a glance at the sleeping woman. Prettiest gal he'd seen in a long time. One that could be dangerous if he were inclined to pursue a relationship. Which he wasn't.

2

A burly man in a top hat and long duster bumped into Tabby. She steadied herself and stepped farther away from the tracks. The din of multiple conversations assaulted her ears until she wanted to put her hands over them. A woman in fancy dress, the bright yellow making her look like a canary, stood on her toes to plant a kiss on a bearded man's cheek. With a shout, the man dashed into the train station depot, clearly energized by the woman's advances.

Tabby could stay and watch the teeming crowd for hours, but instead clutched the bag containing everything she owned. Two dresses, an extra pair of shoes, a hairbrush, her Bible, and a silver comb left to her by her mother. Not to mention the newly signed six-month contract to work for Fred Harvey. There was an option for a year, but she didn't know where she'd be in that length of time. What if she didn't like being one of

Harvey's girls? She shook her head. No, it'd be the perfect job for her. But she wanted to keep her options open.

She thought over the conversation with Mrs. Harvey. She said that the girls garnered multiple marriage proposals. On the other hand, they also received disparaging remarks. But, times were changing, and so would people's outlook on women in the workplace. Tabby felt confident she could help change the way people looked at working women.

Excitement bubbled up, threatening to erupt in a fit of giggles. She'd been deemed perfect to learn the "Harvey way", whatever that meant. She'd pretended to know what Mrs. Harvey was talking about, and prayed it was the type of restaurant Mr. Foster had claimed and not a house of ill repute, or as filthy as her prior employment. The title Harvey Girl still made her nervous, as if she belonged to Fred Harvey instead of being employed by the man.

Please, God, don't let the pastor be right. Don't let my answer to an advertisement land me in a brothel.

Well, if it were a brothel, she wouldn't dare enter, of course. She'd continue on her way, sending her contract back in ripped up pieces. No one took advantage of Tabitha McClelland.

She craned her neck. Still no sign of the train. In moments, she'd be on her way to Topeka, Kansas for training. In her purse, she carried two days' worth of sandwiches and a few pieces of fruit. Of course, the interviewer told her she'd be eating at Harvey houses along the way.

The ground shook, and a whistle split the air. This was it. One step onboard and Tabby's new life would begin. She'd been promised one of the best seats on the train and would travel first class all the way. She couldn't wait for night to fall so she could stretch out in the Pullman car. No more sleeping while sitting, her head bobbing like a baby trying to stay awake at play time.

The train shrieked to a stop. Spewing steam whipped at Tabby's skirt. She stepped back to let passengers disembark.

From fancy dressed men and women to simple farming families, people trooped past her. Some headed into the depot, others into the arms of loved ones. Shouts of greeting filled the air along with the sobs of goodbyes. Sounds Tabby needed to get used to if she'd be working by the train tracks for the next six months. She lifted her dark brown skirt high enough to prevent stumbling and stepped onboard.

After handing her free pass to the conductor, she hurried toward her plush first-class seat. She settled down with a sigh and thought back over her interview.

The meeting with Mrs. Harvey hadn't taken more than fifteen minutes. She'd taken one look at Tabby, studying her from the toes of her freshly polished shoes to her neat hair, asked a few pointed questions about her work experience, seemed thrilled that she despised the railroad diners, and then promptly asked her if she had plans to wed. When Tabby said definitely not, Mrs. Harvey slid a contract across her pine desk and asked her to sign on the dotted line.

It was the easiest thing she'd ever done. She would receive her uniform and first paycheck upon arriving in Topeka, and the other half of her first paycheck at the end of the thirty days of training. Seventeen dollars and fifty cents a month. What would she do with all her money?

As part of the contract, Harvey girls weren't allowed to fraternize with employees of the male persuasion. What, exactly constituted fraternizing? Would she be allowed to speak with the men or did she have to ignore them completely? She shrugged. The details would work themselves out. Tabby clapped her hands, not forgetting the promise of free room and board.

She glimpsed Adam Foster, the chef, on the platform, and patted stray strands of hair in place. Oh, what if he was going to Topeka? Did sharing a train violate a rule? Could she be friends with him? And was he as nice as he seemed, or did Mr. Foster harbor a secret like Pa?

In Tabby's estimation, most men, like her Pa, were after one thing, and one thing only. Something Tabby had no intention of giving. She'd loved her father, but his philandering ways had ruined her family. She wouldn't take such chances with her own future.

She leaned forward as Adam stepped aboard.

A smile spread across his face as he slid onto the seat beside her. "Miss McClelland, it's my pleasure."

Her heart fluttered. "Are you headed to Topeka?"

"Yes. You?" At her nod, he continued. "I'll be chef in one of the finest restaurants in the city, and you'll be the prettiest waitress."

Tabby's cheeks heated. The man did take liberties. He must think her a naïve girl to blush at such a simple compliment. Surely the man jested. Tabby's slight frame and overly large eyes could be called anything but pretty. Or maybe she was reading too much into his words. Most likely he saw a young girl alone and offered his companionship as protection against scoundrels.

She dipped her head. "I am rather excited."

"Maybe you'll become head waitress someday."

"You think so?" A rush of pleasure shot through her. "I'm thinking maybe I'll do my six months, then head farther west and see where the tracks take me."

"You are a true pioneer, aren't you?" Adam extended his legs under the seat in front of them. "Don't you want a family some day?"

She tightened her lips.

He looked apologetic. "I'm sorry. That's none of my business."

Holding her skirt aside, Tabby scooted closer to the wall. They might share a train, but that didn't mean she needed to sit on his lap. The scent of the man's soap tickled her nose and threatened to make her forget her manners. "Harvey girls are not allowed to be married." Come to think of it, she probably wasn't supposed to talk to Adam. But maybe that didn't start until Topeka. Either way, he certainly asked forward questions.

The train lurched ahead, and Tabby transferred her attention out the window. Truth was, his question plagued her. She'd never given much thought to having a family of her own. Life kept her too busy in the struggle for survival. Now that the future looked brighter, would she want to chuck it all away for a husband who would take everything she had? She didn't think so. An independent career woman, that's what Tabitha McClelland wanted to be.

"Your orders, please." A waitress stood beside them, pen poised over a pad of paper.

"For what?" Tabitha clutched her purse. She'd been told all expenses were paid.

"Lunch."

"I brought my own, thank you."

Adam chuckled. "You're about to get your first taste of what you'll be serving." He reached into a pouch in the seat in front of them. "Here's the menu." He glanced at the waitress. "Can you give us a few minutes and take our orders last?"

"Certainly, sir." With a nod, she continued down the aisle and to the next customer.

Tabby grabbed the menu. "This is incredible. They take our orders before we get there?"

"And wire them ahead so they know how many people to serve."

"You mean we'll actually have time to eat?" Amazing.

"You are the funniest girl." Adam smiled over his menu. "Today's lunch is pork with apple sauce. If that isn't to your liking, there are sandwiches served at the lunch counter."

No one had ever called her funny before. She rather liked it. She'd been called stubborn and flighty, but the way Adam said funny things made her feel as if it was a good quality and she was the only girl on the train. Adam Foster could be a dangerous man if he had this much influence on her emotions. She would need to be extra careful with him. She turned back to her menu.

Veal, chicken, even lobster on some days. She'd never had lobster. And the prices were so reasonable for paying customers. Seventy-five cents! "I'll be glad to have the pork with apple sauce and cold custard. Oh, and we get a salad?"

"Yes, ma'am." The waitress smiled. "Whatever you'd like."

"I'll have the same." Adam folded his menu and returned it to the pouch. "Tonight, we'll be having the roast sirloin. Anything they cook will be to your liking, I guarantee it."

She sighed. "I think I've died and gone to heaven."

"Get used to it. This is your life now, and you'll get to order again for dinner."

Goodness, she'd be as big as a cow within a month.

By the time the train rumbled into the station, Tabby's stomach was growling, and her nerves danced.

Adam helped her from the train, and released her hand as soon as they reached the platform. When they entered the restaurant, Tabby put more space between them.

Adam's brow wrinkled. "Do you want to sit at a table or the lunch counter?"

She eyed the stools at the counter. No, best not to sit that close to him. "A table, please." She glanced at him then quickly averted her gaze, not sure whether her skin tickled from anticipation or the way Adam's hand felt as he'd helped steady her. Either way, she liked it, and the thought scared her. She tore her gaze away from him and focused on her surroundings.

Women wearing crisp black dresses and starched white aprons without a spot on them stood next to tables covered with fresh linen tablecloths. Porcelain coffee mugs were placed upside down on ironed cloths. The waitress welcomed her and Adam to their seats and within minutes waitresses quietly placed white salad plates filled with crisp greens and vegetables in front of them.

Tabby couldn't take it all in. By the time she'd finished her salad, a waitress appeared with the main course. It was the most delicious meal Tabby had ever eaten. All served as she hardly said a word. As for her drink, she never mentioned it at all, yet a glass of clear water appeared almost by magic. What a far cry from her previous waitressing experience.

~

Adam enjoyed the look of rapture on Tabby's face as she cut into her meat. Around the room, Harvey girls toted heavy trays laden with food. How would a tiny girl like Tabby fare beneath the weight? Could she hold up to the never-ending pace as the waitresses met the passengers' every need, or would she succumb to illness like his late wife, Marilyn?

Being in the kitchen wouldn't afford him the opportunity to help if things were too difficult for her. He wanted her to succeed and didn't want anything to tarnish her wide-eyed enthusiasm. She reminded him too much of his wife. Sending up a prayer on her behalf, he settled in to enjoy his own meal.

"The meal was wonderful, but I can't eat another bite." Tabby released a deep breath. "I can't remember the last time I could say that."

Adam's heart lurched. Growing up on a farm, he'd rarely gone hungry and pitied those who knew the ache of not having enough to eat. He knew the pain of having few material possessions, and the backbreaking work of farm life, but once he'd saved enough for his own restaurant, the land would be sold and his family would follow him to California. Seemed like a new life out west awaited for just about anyone willing to chase his dream.

"This is a really nice place." Tabby folded her napkin and laid it across her plate.

Adam glanced around the large room filled with comfortable tables and chairs under ambient lighting. A polished wood counter ran the length of one wall where pretty Harvey girls scurried back and forth. "I've heard the location in Topeka is even better. The townsfolk eat there too, not just train passengers. Fred Harvey met a fierce need with his restaurants."

Tabby told him about her last place of employment. Adam couldn't believe people were subjected to such travesty. Not being much of a traveling man until lately, he hadn't experienced such atrocities. His spirits lifted, knowing he'd play a part in making folks' travels on the Santa Fe railroad more pleasant.

Outside, a whistle blew signaling for them to return to the train. Adam crooked his arm and smiled when Tabby placed her small hand on his elbow. He could see the diminutive firecracker as somebody's wife very easily. Just not his. No woman could be that for him again. For now, he'd be content to be her friend.

He led her through the throng of people to their seats. After making sure she was comfortable, he slid in beside her and wished the trip to Kansas would be longer than a couple of days. He couldn't name a single person he'd rather spend time with than Tabby. Her innocent excitement about the world around them helped him see things through new eyes and added to his own excitement. Even the constant soot drifting through the window no longer bothered him. He missed his family. Maybe Tabby could take the place of his younger sister, Darcy, and fill a hole left by loneliness.

"That was absolutely delightful." Tabby's eyes sparkled. "I almost wish it were dinner time already. Oh, then bedtime. I haven't had this much fun in ages."

"I wish I could promise every day will be as wonderful, but unfortunately, work will steal some of that enthusiasm."

"Don't say that. I believe I'm going to the best job in the world." She waved her arms. "Did you see how happy the Harvey girls were? Always smiling. Not a cross word out of any of them."

He hadn't the heart to tell her that anything less would most likely result in instant dismissal, or at the minimum a stern reprimand.

~

Tabby donned her flannel nightclothes and climbed under the fresh smelling sheets of her bunk. What a wonderful day. Adam's company couldn't be bested. She stared at the ceiling and dwelled on his bluebonnet eyes, hair the color of mahogany, and his square jaw. Easily the most handsome man she'd met in her life. Made only better by the fact he was such a gentleman. At least he appeared so on the outside. But as she knew only too well, appearances were often deceiving.

Tears stung her eyes. Ma would've loved him.

Soft footsteps sounded outside her door, and Tabby clutched the sheet closer to her chin. She peered through the dim light to make sure she'd slid the latch. So far, no one had tried to accost her on the train, but experience had taught her that the night often brought out the bad in people. Under the cover of darkness, they tried all kinds of diabolical deeds. She shuddered. At this rate, she'd never get to sleep.

"Miss McClelland?" The conductor's whisper drifted through the door. "Is everything to your liking?"

"Yes," she squeaked. "Thank you."

"Good night, then." His footsteps faded away.

Could folks be more considerate? She didn't think so. Tabby's fears evaporated. Nothing evil would befall her with the conductor roaming the halls, and Adam sleeping just a few doors away.

During the last couple of years, Tabby's faith in a loving God who watched over her had faltered. But more days like today would go far in rekindling a fire in her spirit.

The Harvey girls worked hard, no doubt about it, but Tabby was used to tough work. Having a job she loved would be a first, and no soft-spoken warnings from Adam would change that. No sirree.

More people passed outside her door. She assumed they were passengers without a comfortable berth to stretch out in who had chosen to stretch their legs. Tabby whispered a soft prayer of thanksgiving. She wasn't sure whether God heard her anymore, but a lifetime of prayer was hard to break. If He did hear, she wanted Him to know how much she appreciated the turn her life had taken.

She counted Adam as the first of the many friends she would make. No longer would she fear the night or feel alone even in the midst of people. She'd work hard and move up the ranks until she was number one. The interviewer had mentioned the girls were given numbers to signify their rank, and as they worked, the numbers lowered until they became head waitress. Wouldn't that be grand!

Mrs. Harvey cautioned that men often snatched up the girls, sometimes before they'd fulfilled their contracts. Well, that wouldn't happen to Tabby.

The click-clack of the train's wheels lulled her to sleep. She dreamed she wore the head waitress uniform.

COOKING WITH LOVE

3

"Welcome to Harvey House." A dark-haired woman wearing a pleated skirt the color of ink and a spotless white blouse that sported a black ribbon at her throat stood on the top step leading into the building. She folded her hands in front of her and stared down at Tabby and two other young women. A small smile that didn't quite reach her eyes tugged at the corners of her mouth. "I am Miss O'Connor, the head waitress here. Please follow me."

Tabby glanced at the pale-faced girl walking beside her, and said, "I'm as nervous as a long-tailed cat in a room full of rocking chairs. Everything seems so perfect and businesslike." She held out her hand. "I'm Tabby McClelland."

The girl returned her handshake. "Abigail Smythe, and I completely share your sentiment." She giggled and clapped a hand over her mouth.

Tabby liked the auburn-haired girl immediately. Her infectious laugh went a long way toward relieving Tabby's fears.

The other girl, with hair the color of corn silk, leaned around Abigail. "I'm Ingrid. I, too, am very nervous."

"Move faster, ladies. We have a lot to do today." Miss O'Connor cast a stern look over her shoulder. "We don't allow dawdling."

Tabby and Abigail lifted their skirts and increased their pace, their shoes slapping against the platform. Tabby barely had time to register the polished wood floors, starched tablecloths, sparkling glassware, and girls in the noticeable Harvey uniform, before she and the other two were whisked up a back staircase to the third floor.

They entered a large room filled with racks of black dresses and starched aprons, and a white-haired woman waved them forward. "Come. We must fit you for your uniforms. These must be kept spotless at all times." She lifted a black dress from a hanger. "If you soil your dress or your apron, it must be changed immediately. No excuses. You wear a black ribbon tied at the neck, and a white bow in your hair."

"That'll be a lot of laundry," Abigail said.

"Don't be silly, girl." Miss O'Connor squinted at Abigail with an irritated flicker in her eyes. "Mr. Harvey doesn't require his waitresses to do their own laundry. We send it all out to be taken care of." She sniffed. "I do hope you won't be a complainer."

Tabby grinned. What would there be to complain about? They'd be treated like queens. She couldn't believe her good fortune.

Miss O'Connor pulled three tags from a shelf. "We

work on a points system. Each of you will start at number 14. As you do a good job, points will be taken off. I made it to number one in less than a year. I expect no less from my girls."

She pulled a clipboard from a nail on the wall. "Tabitha McClelland and Abigail Smythe will share room three. Ingrid Schultz, you will bunk with one of our older girls in room two. Please report promptly to me in one hour to begin your training." She turned on her heel and left.

"Roommates." Tabby clapped her hands. She'd made a friend and prayed they'd be like sisters.

The older woman chuckled. "Don't mind Miss O'Connor. I'm Mrs. Moore, the seamstress. Been working here since my beloved Ezra passed away a year ago. Miss O'Connor's bark is often worse than her bite. But she does run a tight ship. Mr. Hastings, the manager, is worse. But don't let me be scaring you girls none." She held up a pair of uniforms. "There's a story to be told there, but I've yet to find it. Try these on." She handed each of them a uniform.

"I'm good at sizing a girl by looking at her, but once in a while I make a mistake, and you're a scrawny thing," she said to Tabby. "Mark your uniforms someway so you can retrieve them later. The basket for soiled clothing is in the corner. Quickly, girls. You still need to unpack, and the wagon boss doesn't tolerate tardiness."

"Wagon boss?" Tabby asked. My, that sounded harsh.

"Head waitress. Same thing." Mrs. Moore smiled. "But don't let her hear you call her Wagon Boss. Now scoot."

"Yes, ma'am." Tabby scurried down the hall and to her room. Her carpetbag waited for her on one of two single-sized beds. A four-drawer oak dresser sat between the beds. An oval mirror hung above it. One window relieved the starkness of the wall. Tabby rushed over and peered out.

Several people meandered up and down the train platform. Tabby raised the window and closed her eyes against the gentle breeze. Murmurs of conversations filled the air. The morning sun stretched long shadows along the wooden planks.

"What are you doing?" Abigail pulled her back. "We have to get dressed. There isn't much time."

Tabby sighed. "You're right. But days on a train left me wanting a breath of fresh air and to feel the sun on my face."

"You most likely won't be feeling that except for Sunday afternoons." Abigail let her traveling dress fall to the floor and slipped into her uniform.

Tabby rushed to follow suit. Some of her previous enthusiasm had waned at the stern appearance of Miss O'Connor, but Tabby vowed not to let a sour woman's attitude ruin her adventure. She sat on the bed to roll up her new stockings. When was the last time she wore stockings that didn't have holes or runs in them?

"Come on!" Abigail dashed out the door.

With a last glance at the open window, Tabby rushed after her. They met Ingrid in the hall, and the three girls headed downstairs.

At the sight of them, Miss O'Connor pulled a pocket watch from her waistband and scowled. Without another word, she led them to a small room off the kitchen.

Tabby caught a glimpse of Adam stirring a huge copper pot and her heart fluttered. Would she ever get used to seeing his handsome features? She took one last look at his broad back then stepped through the doorway Miss O'Connor had disappeared into.

"Girls, once I've gone over the rules, you will be assigned to follow and work alongside a more experienced waitress until the time you are deemed capable of working without close supervision." She lifted her chin.

"You must always uphold a strict moral code. There is no fraternizing with male customers or employees. This includes the workmen on the railroad. You may not sit down while serving customers. No makeup, no jewelry, and absolutely no gum chewing." She let her gaze settle momentarily on each girl. Tabby did her best not to squirm.

"We set a high standard for our girls here at Harvey House. Should you find the time for courting, which I doubt, Mrs. Moore or myself will act as chaperone. The breaking of any of these rules can result in immediate dismissal. Remember, all three of you have the number fourteen, as new girls should. If you do well, you can move up the ranks to lower numbers. Are there any questions before you begin?"

Abigail leaned close and whispered. "I've heard despite the rules, many girls find husbands. I know I plan to."

"Is there something you'd like to share, Miss Smythe? Miss McClelland?"

Tabby shook her head and prayed she could remember all the rules. Her previous excitement had drained like sand through an hourglass. Regardless, she promised herself she'd never give a reason for her job to be jeopardized. In fact, she'd be number one by the end of her contract or die trying. She wouldn't give the snooty head waitress any reason to doubt her work ethic or moral standards. Tabby straightened her shoulders and returned the woman's stare.

Besides, with all the restrictions about who *not* to fraternize with, how did a woman find a man to court her anyway?

~

Adam didn't miss Tabby's passing by the kitchen. The air practically shimmered with her presence. He'd read the rules posted on the wall. They applied to him, same as anyone else. He stirred the hollandaise sauce with all the attention of a gnat. Not good. It'd be his head if he burned the fixings for lunch.

He liked the idea of the menu planned far enough in advance that frequent travelers could rely on a varied menu while traveling. Today's lunch was sliced ham with asparagus. The diversity wouldn't allow boredom for him or the passengers. Adam sniffed, breathing in the warm yeasty scent of baked bread.

"Josiah, is the bread ready to come out of the oven? The train will be here in an hour." Adam motioned for one of his assistants to stop ogling the waitresses and get back to work.

"Right away, sir." The wiry young man leaped to do Adam's bidding. Grabbing a thick towel, he pulled a pan of loaves from the large oven.

Adam eyed the browned mounds. "Perfect. Good job." He moved the pan of sauce to a back burner and checked the meat. It'd be ready right on time. He could use the next few minutes to start the salads. First opportunity he got, he'd ask why he didn't have another assistant or two. Hard to be productive with little help.

Light footfalls on the stairs alerted him that one of the waitresses had arrived for work. His heart lifted at the sight of Tabby in her uniform. As modest as the dress was, her beauty shone through. "Miss McClelland, you look lovely today."

She curtsied, her cheeks darkening. "Thank you, Mr. Foster."

They both turned at the sound of someone clearing his throat. Oh, no. Adam met the hard gaze of Mr. Hastings, the restaurant manager.

The man straightened his bony shoulders and stared down his long nose. "There is no fraternizing between help. Do not let it happen again."

"Sir, I only greeted—"

"Rules are rules, Mr. Foster." The man strode through the kitchen and into the dining room.

Adam glanced at the tearful eyes of Tabby and mouthed, "I'm sorry."

She nodded and scurried out of sight.

"Don't let Mr. Hastings bother you none. He's a masher, always after the girls, but none of them will let him court." Josiah slid out the last pan of bread and set it on the wood counter with a clatter. "Nobody dares complain against him for fear of losing their jobs, but there's rumors that him and the lemon sucking head mistress sometimes meet up after hours. The rest of the girls escape him by getting hitched."

Adam chopped tomatoes into wedges. Two more waitresses glided into the kitchen in search of rags to wipe tables. He avoided their glances.

Mr. Hastings chased the girls? Had rendezvous' with

O'Connor? Adam shook his head, wanting nothing more than to stay out of work politics, save his money, pack up his family, and head to California. That's what he'd focus on.

Soon, salad bowls lined the workspace. The reds and greens of the vegetables provided a nice contrast with the white porcelain. He glanced around the up-to-date kitchen. This wasn't the first restaurant Adam had cooked for, but it was the nicest. He couldn't believe his fortune. Everyone had heard of Fred Harvey's newest venture. Some applauded his efforts, others laughed, at least in the beginning, saying the man would lose his shirt. Adam never dreamed he'd be involved in such an undertaking.

Tabby scooted around another girl, nodded in Adam's direction without making eye contact, and grabbed napkin wrapped silverware. High spots of crimson dotted each fair cheek.

Adam smiled. She wasn't unaffected by him, despite the averting of her glance.

~

Tabby paused to catch her breath and leaned against the wall. From the moment she came downstairs after donning her uniform, she'd flitted from one workstation to another like a black and white hummingbird. She hurriedly tucked flyaway strands of hair back into its bow. It wouldn't do to be reprimanded again on the first day, especially for her appearance.

"If customers aren't waiting, there's a dining room to be dusted, also silverware to be rolled and napkins to be folded. There's no end to work, Miss McClelland." Miss O'Connor sailed by, her arms full of folded linens. "No dawdling."

With a sigh, Tabby pushed away from the wall and shuffled back to work.

If she thought she was busy before, the first train load of passengers caused a whirlwind of activity. By the time folks were in the door, each waitress waited calmly by a table, arms seemingly relaxed at their sides and a smile on each girl's face. Tabby's nerves jumped like frog legs in a hot skillet.

"Relax." Mary, the girl Tabby was assigned to follow, smiled down at her. "The work's hard, but rewarding, and the passengers hardly complain. They're happy to get a quality meal. You watch me this time, then later you can work the coffee machine at the lunch counter. Once training is complete, you'll have an easier job than waitressing."

"All right." Tabby took a deep breath and pasted a smile on her face. She could do this. The twelve hour days were worth the future of adventure in the West and the thrill of meeting new people and hearing their stories.

A family of six sat at the table assigned to Mary. The children's excited chatter rose above the gentle clinking of silverware as the napkins were unrolled and voices murmured in soft conversation. Tabby stood to the side as Mary greeted them, poured water and coffee, then moved to the kitchen to get their salads, all without breaking stride or losing her smile.

Tabby followed. Would she be as efficiently pleasant as the other girls seemed to be? Were they as happy on the inside as they appeared on the outside? What if a customer grew irate? Miss O'Connor didn't tell them what to do then. Tabby's head ached from all the questions.

Although the thrill of working in such a nice establishment filled her, she couldn't help but realize her last job, however messy, had been easy. She pushed open the kitchen door.

A movement caught her eye, and she glanced down. A mouse skittered across the toe of her shiny black shoe.

4

Tabby shrieked and leaped to the closest object above the floor, the kitchen counter. A pan of white sauce crashed to the floor, its contents splashing across the sparkling tile. A drop burned Tabby's skin through her wool stockings.

Mary squawked and clasped a hand over her mouth as she backpedaled from the room.

Adam whirled, brandishing a wooden spoon like a weapon. "What is it?"

"A mouse." Tabby pointed behind a small table with wheels. Goosebumps crawled up her spine.

Adam laughed. "You're afraid of a little four-legged creature?"

"Don't jest. Kill it!" She tucked her legs under her long skirt.

"What is going on in here?" Mr. Hastings stormed into the kitchen, eyebrows raised and hands on his hips.

"Miss McClelland! Get off the counter this instant."

"But, Mr. Hastings, there's a—" She clamped her lips together at Adam's fierce shake of his head and hid her trembling hands in the folds of her apron.

"A what?" He snapped his fingers, motioning for her to get down.

Tabby gulped and slid off the counter. "A mouse, sir."

"Impossible." His took a deep breath. "Mice are not allowed in Mr. Harvey's restaurant. I will be letting Miss O'Connor know of your shameful behavior. Of that there is no doubt."

Lump in her throat, Tabby's shoulders slumped. Averting her eyes from Adam and the young man already at work cleaning up her mess, she lifted her skirts and carefully made her way back to the dining room.

"The water, Miss McClelland." Miss O'Conner scowled.

Oh! That's why she had gone into the kitchen. She turned and dashed back for the wheeled cart with pitchers of fresh water. She slipped on the spilled sauce, wind-milled her arms, continued her slide past the cart, and came to a crashing halt against Adam's chest. His strong hands steadied her. Heavens.

"Are you all right, Tabby?"

She was anything but. Especially with his arms around her, which was entirely inappropriate and could get them both reprimanded no matter how innocent. Still avoiding his gaze, she rested her forehead against his solid chest, just for a moment while she caught her breath, then nodded.

Willing her heartbeat to return to normal, she guided

the cart into the dining room. What could Adam possibly be thinking of her ridiculous behavior? Other than his laugh, and her insane response, she hadn't looked his way again. But it had felt good to have him hold her. She shoved away the foolish thoughts. She was a Harvey Girl. Work came first.

She rolled the cart to where the other waitresses stood, and waited while each took a pitcher. This day might be her first, and last, once Mr. Hastings had a chance to talk to Miss O'Connor. She prayed she was wrong.

Needing to think of a way to redeem herself, she gave a faint smile and took up her position next to Mary at their table.

"What happened in there? Was that a mouse I saw?" Mary glanced toward the door. "Mr. Hastings came from the kitchen perfectly livid."

Tabby squared her shoulders. "We'll talk later."

"There's a spot of Hollandaise on your shoe." Mrs. O'Connor stopped next to her. "Clean it at the first opportunity. We do not condone slovenly appearances."

Tabby groaned as her smile faded. The head waitress condoned very little, and now Tabby had another strike against her. Her hopes of adventure in the west were dying by the minute. If she lost her job, she would have no funds available for a trip to anywhere.

Mary waited for the head waitress to move on. "Don't worry. You'll be fine. Families are the easiest to please. Much better than a society lady on her own who tends to be demanding. No one will notice your shoe."

"I pray so." Tabby stepped forward. "Welcome to Harvey's. My name is Tabitha and I will be serving you today."

"Thank you." The woman sat. The look on her face seemed apologetic. "My brood does tend to be rowdy, and I'm at my wit's end." She waved a hand. "It will be nice to have someone else deal with them for half an hour."

Tabby feigned a smile. She turned from the woman to Mary with wide eyes and a silent plea for help. Mary nodded toward the table where plates of crisp salad sat in front of each customer. She'd been so flustered with the mouse she hadn't noticed Mary return to the kitchen for the salads. Gracious, she hoped the other waitress hadn't seen her in Adam's arms.

"May I please take your drink orders?" Tabby folded her hands.

"I'll have the coffee." The gentleman nodded. "My wife, tea, and the children, milk."

Tabby hurried to turn their cups to the proper positions so the drink girl would know who ordered what. "Someone will have those to you directly. I will see to your meals." She gave a slight bow and backed away. Whew. That wasn't too hard. She hurried to the manager and waited while he cut thick slices of ham to be added to the plates.

"Quickly, ladies," he warned. "The food must be served hot. Miss McClelland, please fetch me another platter."

"Yes, sir." Tabby rushed through the kitchen doors. "More meat!"

Adam handed her a platter.

She hadn't expected such a load. Surprise crossed her face as she grunted under its weight.

"Can you carry that?" Adam reached out.

"Of course." It wouldn't do to add dropping a slab of

ham to her sins of the day. Hefting it higher, she struggled back to the dining room and plopped it next to Mr. Hastings.

"A little more finesse, please." He waved his butcher knife, his voice rising above the clatter of the patrons. "Now, see to your table."

Must he embarrass her so? She managed to do that quite well on her own.

Tabby nodded, grabbed her customer's plates, and rushed back to her table. By the time the train left, perspiration dotted her brow and her shoulders ached. It was only lunchtime. How would she make it through dinner?

~

Compassion for Tabby filled Adam. His heart rate ticked up a notch as he cleaned the stove. Was it thoughts of her or the physical labor she endured? First the mouse incident, then the crazy slide across the floor and smacking into him, and finally the heavy meat platter. He grinned, remembering the way her face reddened. What a day she'd had. If only he could help her. His gaze landed on the posted rules. His shoulders slumped. He'd find a way.

"Josiah," Adam waved his hand. "Find that mouse hole and plug it, will you? We can't have a repeat of this morning. I'm sure Miss McClelland isn't the only lady with an aversion to rodents." They weren't his favorite critter either, especially in the kitchen.

"Yes, sir."

Adam reviewed the dinner menu and wondered how Tabby fared after the lunch rush. A lot of customers brought their own mid-day meal, making the noon hour less hectic than dinner. He'd heard no more roars of disapproval from the manager or the "wagon boss", so he hoped Tabby's morning fiascos hadn't gotten her fired.

Many girls made mistakes in their first days. Tabby's were minor compared to what could have happened—like a full plate of hot gravy in someone's lap. He grinned. If that disaster were to happen to anyone, it would be to her.

"May I have a rag, please?" The diminutive girl had snuck up on him. "I have a spot of sauce on my shoe."

He handed her a clean rag. Exhaustion clouded her fair features. "Sit for a minute. You look like you'll fall over at the slightest provocation. Not that I'm averse to picking you up, but it wouldn't look right to the others."

"Please don't tease after this morning's embarrassing episode. I apologize for my forwardness." She dropped to a straight back chair. "Whew, I've never worked so hard in all my life." She bent to wipe her shoe. "I swear my body hates me." She straightened with a red face. "I hope I don't sound ungrateful for the work or your concern. I assure you I'm not."

"No, just honest." He leaned against the counter, admiring the way her hair escaped its bow and curled around her face. "Can I get you a drink of water?"

"I would love one, but please hurry." She glanced toward the door. "I can't take too long."

Adam fetched a glass and filled it from a pitcher. "Twelve hour shifts can wear a person down. You have to take breaks."

"I can't. Not after this morning." She took a gulp and handed it back to him. "Thank you. I must get back before I'm missed." She fluttered out the door like a runaway sparrow.

"You shouldn't flit around her." Josiah straightened from behind the counter. "You know the rules."

"Yeah, I do." Adam tossed the rag into the laundry. "I just gave her a drink. That shouldn't be against anyone's rules. Besides, I've seen you ogle the ladies when you sneak out back for a smoke."

Josiah grinned. "The ladies do like a bad boy. But you don't seem the type. Just telling you to be careful. I saw your face when you held her this morning."

"I'll be careful." Adam cast another glance toward the door, hoping to catch another glimpse of the girl he shouldn't be talking to. Not only did the rules discourage relationships, but a pretty face could halt his dream in its tracks.

The door opened again and Tabby peered in. "We're out of clean silverware."

"I'll get it, Miss." Josiah ducked into the pantry. "Dishwasher didn't show up again. Means I'll have to wash. I hate washing."

Adam grinned at his complaining. "Better chance of you keeping your job."

Tabby gripped the edge of the open door. "Wish I had that. I haven't heard from Miss O'Connor yet. What is she waiting for?"

"The fox isn't after the chickens yet. Don't worry without cause."

"Right." She backed out.

"You have that look again." Josiah appeared with a tray of clean utensils.

"What look?" Adam dropped the evening's menu in the sink of dishwater.

"Like the sun just went behind a cloud."

"Shut up." He fished the soggy paper from the water

and spread it on the counter. The ink had run, but was still legible. Tonight they would serve braised duck. He'd better get his mind on work.

He chuckled and sent up a prayer that Miss O'Connor wouldn't fire Tabby. Life would be interesting with Miss McClelland around, and Adam felt they could both use a friend.

5

"Miss McClelland, my room, please." Miss O'Connor turned and marched down the hall, her heels clacking out Tabby's doom.

"Good luck," Abigail said, removing the pins from her hair.

"Thanks." Tabby laid her hairbrush on top of her dresser, and quickly tied her hair off her neck. "I have a feeling I'm going to need it."

"Don't fret." Abigail smiled. "I won't give your bed away just yet."

What would she do if she were fired? Tears stung Tabby's eyes. Exhaustion weighted her limbs, yet she forced her head high. She would not cow under the head waitress's stern gaze. *Lord, give me strength.*

She'd dawdled too long making herself presentable, most likely adding another demerit to the list Miss O'Connor probably had sitting on her desk. But, she couldn't have dashed off right away with her hair in disarray. Not unless she wanted the wagon boss to die of apoplexy.

Tabby stopped at the threshold of Miss O'Connor's room, took a deep breath, and knocked. The door was open, but she knew the woman stood on strict propriety and would not appreciate someone entering without permission.

"Come in and close the door, please." Miss O'Connor sat behind a simple wood desk, hands folded in front of her, a pair of spectacles perched low on her nose.

With trembling hands, Tabby did as instructed. She released the breath she'd been holding, then turned to face the wagon boss.

Miss O'Connor laid the glasses on the desktop, and sighed. "I am grievously disappointed in you, Miss McClelland." She tapped a sheet of paper with her index finger. "You came with high recommendations from Mrs. Harvey herself. Seems you made quite an impression on her during your interview. I must confess, I don't see what she saw in you."

Tabby swallowed against the mountain in her throat and begged her legs not to fold. She felt seconds away from being fired. Lord, make it painless. She blinked back tears and focused on a dark spot on the wall above Miss O'Connor's head. "What do you see, Miss?" Oh, why couldn't she hold her tongue?

"I see an impertinent girl who thinks her job is something to be ridiculed." Miss O'Connor planted her palms flat on the desk top and pushed to her feet. Mr. Hastings came to me after the dinner hour with a ridiculous story of you perched on a counter." She took a sharp breath. "As if that were not enough, one of the other girls came to me with an eyewitness account of you being hugged by our chef. Miss McClelland, I don't know what lifestyle you came from, but—"

Tabby opened her mouth, then clamped her lips tight and bit her tongue. Let the woman think what she wanted. Tabby didn't need the approval of anyone but God. She had done nothing wrong with Adam and would not apologize for it.

Apparently Miss O'Connor saw her attempt at speech. She paused for a moment, giving Tabby time to answer. When she didn't, the woman continued. "We have strict guidelines here. I'm afraid I must give you a mark for today's performance. At this rate, you won't drop in ranking very quickly. I hope you do better with the rest of your training. The other girls are bypassing you with their efficiency. You may leave," she said with a dismissive flip of her wrist.

Did she say Tabby was inefficient? She went to bed each evening bone weary, doing twice as much work as the other girls. But wait. Tabby blinked. "You aren't firing me?"

"Not just yet, Miss McClelland. Keep up the shoddy work, and I'll have no other option but to release you from your duties." Miss O'Connor positioned the glasses back on her face and slid the paper from her desk into a drawer. She sighed. "I am not so naïve as to think that the ladies keep strictly to the rule about no fraternizing, but please, if you insist on jeopardizing your moral standing, please be discreet. Good night."

Tabby forced her rubbery legs to carry her out the door. Once in the hall, she leaned against the wall and closed her eyes. Her heart was beating faster than the wheels on the train that had brought her there. How many warnings did a girl get before being fired? Maybe she hadn't performed as bad as she thought. After all, her behavior had been completely respectable. Or maybe God still had work and further adventure for her at Harvey's Topeka Restaurant. Despite the reprimand from her boss, she couldn't wait to see what the future held.

The clock downstairs gonged nine, signaling she had one hour left before curfew. Without a second thought, Tabby dashed downstairs and out the kitchen's back door.

The cool night breeze washed over her, drying her tears. She took a deep breath and sat on the stoop. Maybe she should make this a nightly ritual, at least until winter set in. A time to unwind and watch the stars after a hard day's work. A few moments of precious solitude after a busy restaurant and a chattering roommate.

She leaned back against the still-warm brick of the building. Receiving a mark hadn't deterred her determination to seek adventure and move every six months down the Santa Fe line. If anything, it strengthened it. God wouldn't have given her a spirit for adventure if she weren't to pursue it, would He? No, she wouldn't get attached to this place.

What had the head waitress meant about being discreet? Were Tabby's morals in question because Adam had prevented her from taking a nasty fall? Surely not. Would the woman rather Tabby had fallen to the hard tile floor and possibly suffered injury?

The door opened. Kitchen light flowed out into the darkness, outlining Adam's frame. Tabby's breath hitched. She tucked her trembling hands into the folds of her skirt. No matter how much she convinced herself she had no time for romance, the man did things to her heart that no other man ever had. Things that left her confused and scared.

No, she couldn't get attached to Kansas or any person there. She was strong willed. It shouldn't be too difficult to ignore the way her blood raced when the handsome chef walked by.

~

"Good evening, Tabby. Mind if I join you?" Adam shut the door quietly behind him.

"Of course not, if you don't think we'll be in trouble."

"Why would I be in trouble for taking out the garbage?" He grinned and set the garbage pail on the ground before lowering himself beside her, their shoulders touching in the confined space of the step. "Have you heard from the wagon boss yet?"

"Yes." Her soft answer led him to believe the worst.

"I'm sorry. It won't be the same around here without you." He wasn't sure which hurt more, knowing she was leaving, or the fact that he would care. He reached for her hand, then was reminded of the intimacy of the gesture and folded his hands in his lap instead.

She laughed, a light breathless sound that sent tingles up his spine. "I wasn't fired, just reprimanded. Seems one of the other girls saw my outlandish behavior with you in the kitchen, and Miss O'Connor thought the worst."

"Did you explain that you slipped and almost fell?"

He felt a warm sensation from her shrug against his shoulder. "No. The woman will believe what she wants." She shifted. "I didn't feel the need to clarify a situation that didn't warrant it. If I had explained, she would have thought I was arguing with her or covering up some worse sin with my denial. I'm only here until my contract expires, so I'll try hard not to let Miss O'Connor's personal feelings about me affect me overly much."

Adam felt suddenly alone although only inches separated them. He wasn't sure how he felt about her strong desire to leave. "I, for one, am glad you're staying. At least for now."

"Thank you, although I fear it isn't wise for us to form a friendship." She stood. "Others will think the worst. If it's a woman you're looking for, there is a courting parlor, but I'm afraid it will have to be someone else."

Adam jumped to his feet and laid a hand on her arm. "Please, I wish only to be friends. I'm not looking to get married." No, he'd tried that before and all it had left him with was a broken heart.

"Good, I could use a friend more than a suitor." With a swish of her skirts, she rushed into the kitchen.

Spirit light, Adam retrieved his garbage pail and set off across the yard to the larger can. He made a mental note to return to the steps tomorrow night at the same time. Maybe it could become a time for him and Tabby to talk about their day. A peaceful end to each busy day.

"Tsk tsk, Adam." The glow of a cigarette alerted him to Josiah's presence. "Did you choose not to heed my advice?"

"Just taking out the garbage." He put a hand on the doorknob. Why did the other man care? He chased after all the waitresses. Why should he bother Adam about spending time with just one. A very special one, at that.

"With a pretty little gal. Best be careful, my friend. You could get burned."

6

Tabby lifted a fork and turned it this way and that, checking for smudges and water drops. The lantern's light glinted off the polished silver showing it to be impeccably cleaned.

Miss O'Connor seemed inclined to give Tabby the less desirable chores, making her start earlier and end later. Mama, bless her soul, used to say hard work built character. Tabby wasn't always inclined to agree with her. Moments like this, she felt she had all the character she needed.

After a month, Ingrid already had two points taken off her card, and Abigail one. Both girls had a better grasp at being a good Harvey Girl, it seemed, than Tabby. She was the only one still left at fourteen. She sighed. Maybe she wasn't cut out for this kind of work. She'd done her best curbing her tongue and keeping her opinions to herself. Maybe she shouldn't. The next time

Miss O'Connor came down hard on Tabby, she'd straighten her shoulders and stand up for herself.

Sure, she would, right before she received the last of her pay.

Most likely the spilled sauce had something to do with her points not changing. Maybe someone tattled about her regular conversations with Adam on the back stoop most nights. She shrugged and rolled the spotless fork in an equally spotless napkin and then reached for another.

"Hurry up, Miss McClelland, the breakfast crowd will be here soon." Miss O'Connor breezed past. "It won't do to not have silverware on the tables. Our guests cannot eat with their hands."

"Yes, ma'am." If not for the nightly conversations with Adam, Tabby would be tempted to give up. She could probably find work in a larger city. She glanced out the front window. Maybe San Francisco would offer plenty of job opportunities, along with the adventure Tabby craved. No, quitting before the end of her contract was unethical, something Tabby was proud to say she wasn't.

The train whistle blew, signaling the arrival of the day's first customers. Tabby tossed a spoon onto the counter, hefted the wicker basket with the rolled silverware, then scurried to place a set at each table setting. After placing the basket back behind the counter, she rushed to take a stand beside her assigned table, and struggled to regulate her breathing. All she did was run, it seemed. She glanced at the head waitress.

Where was the kind motherly figure some of the girls talked about other wagon bosses being? Many of them were as discouraged as Tabby by the constant barking of orders by Miss O'Conner. Was the way she ran things not the norm? Could Tabby possibly request a transfer?

She glanced toward the kitchen where Adam was cooking breakfast. And lose the best friend she'd ever had? No, she couldn't. Not yet. She did still crave adventure, and this stop was the first of many, she hoped. She would miss Adam. She would have to think long and hard about moving on when her contract here was done.

She straightened her shoulders. She would do her job to the best of her ability and let God handle the details. If only she weren't so tired all the time.

Smile in place, she welcomed the guests and took their orders. Someday, she'd be the drink girl and have to carry nothing heavier than a pitcher, nor remember anything more difficult than which way a cup was turned. Meal orders in hand, she dashed to the kitchen. "Two pancake platters, please."

Adam stood pouring batter onto a hot griddle. His assistants, the same young man who was there when Tabby started working, and the new boy, poured syrup into glass bottles and placed slabs of butter on china butter dishes.

"Are you all right?" Adam studied her face. "You look pale. You're working too hard."

She waved him off. "I'll be fine. I just ran from the front of the restaurant."

He narrowed his eyes, clearly not believing her. "Maybe you should take a day off. Let Miss O'Connor know you're ill."

And let the woman have another strike against

Tabby? No, thank you. Tomorrow marked the end of her training period, and she would no longer have another waitress hovering over her shoulder all day. "Please, don't concern yourself about me."

Tomorrow was Sunday. She could rest all afternoon after church.

"I can't help—" He turned back to the stove when the door opened behind Tabby.

"Miss McClelland, must I always search for you?" Miss O'Conner glared. "With your training almost over, I would like nothing more than to give you high recommendations."

Tabby grabbed the pancake plates. "It won't happen again." She ducked her head and rushed back to the waiting customers. Tears pricked her eyes. She couldn't do anything right in the head waitress's eyes. Her head grew light. Maybe she was ill. No, she couldn't be. There wasn't time. It was nothing but nerves. Not that Tabby was normally a nervous person, but working under the scrutiny of Miss O'Connor would stretch anyone to the breaking point.

The constant criticism ate at Tabby. There had to be a way for her to win Miss O'Connor's approval, something other than just hard work and a good work ethic.

Once the breakfast crowd was gone, Tabby headed to the washroom. Ignoring her glassy eyes in the mirror, she splashed cool water on her face. Hopefully, the cleansing would rejuvenate her so she could get through the day. She planted her hands on the basin and stared at her reflection.

High spots of color on her cheeks signified a fever. Tabby wasn't sure which she would prefer; an illness or exhaustion. Either one would keep her from working. She closed her eyes. *Please, God, keep me moving. Don't let me succumb to weakness.*

~

Tabby sighed and glanced at the clock. Finally, quitting time. She bypassed the kitchen door. Unfortunately, there was no energy for a conversation with Adam. Every bone in her body ached.

The stairs stretched on forever, taking the last ounce of strength she had to climb to her room. She waved off Abigail's questions, disrobed, and slid into bed in her slip. The thick quilt failed to prevent shivers, and weighed heavy on her aching limbs.

"I'm telling Miss O'Connor." Abigail stormed from the room, leaving Tabby to cringe and wish she could shut out the world.

Way too soon, the head waitress and Abigail returned. Miss O'Connor rushed into the room. She laid a cool hand against Tabby's forehead.

"Why, she's burning up." She snapped her fingers. "Fetch me a basin of cool water and a clean cloth. Tabitha, why didn't you tell me you were ill?"

"I didn't want it to reflect badly on my review." Tears scalded a path down her cheeks, wetting her pillow.

Moments later, Abigail reappeared with the requested items and set them on the small table beside Tabby's bed.

"Leave us, please." Miss O'Connor placed a cool rag across Tabby's forehead. "Miss McClelland. I am hard on all my girls, but I am not in the habit of doing it in front of others, so some feel I am harsher with them than I am with another. You most likely feel you are the only one I am this way with." She dipped the rag back in the basin. "You are easily the best waitress we have." She smiled. "You remind me of myself when I first started. Like me, you will make a wonderful wagon boss. In order to do so, you need to know every aspect of the job, from the lowest duty to the highest."

"But I'm still at fourteen. The others—"

"Will not be chosen first when another restaurant needs a fill-in. You, Tabitha, will be the one sent. These are the reasons I am so hard on you." Miss O'Connor stood. "I will retire to my room. Abigail will come for me if you worsen. Most likely you are suffering from a cold. Thank goodness tomorrow is Sunday. If you have not recuperated by Monday, you will stay in bed, and I will call the doctor."

Miss O'Conner glided from the room. The woman's show of tenderness left Tabby unsure and confused. She was hard on the girls because she cared about them? Tabby was her best waitress? She fell asleep with her mind whirling and feeling as if the last month had been nothing but a strange dream.

~

Adam took out the garbage then sat on the stoop as usual. At least what he thought was usual. Tabby hadn't shown up the last few nights and tonight he was worried about her. Especially after how ill she looked earlier.

Then one of the other girls came down asking for water and a rag. He glanced up at the row of windows where the women's rooms were. How he wished he could check on Tabby, but unless he wanted both of them to lose their jobs, that would not be a smart move. He leaned his elbows on his knees, hands dangling between them, and stared at the ground.

Marilyn's death had started with nothing more threatening than a fever. Since then, any type of illness in someone Adam cared about sent streams of ice through his veins.

Only after knowing her one month, Tabby mattered more to him than he deemed wise. His life didn't allow for a woman to occupy his thoughts and threaten to divert him from his goal. Maybe in a few years, but definitely not yet. His family was as eager as he was to open a restaurant in San Francisco. Adam couldn't let them down by losing his job. The sale of their farm wouldn't give them enough funds for the trek west and opening their own restaurant.

He kicked at a rock in the dirt and decided to go to bed. Even if Tabby wasn't sick, it couldn't be a good idea to continue their night time visits. His heart ached at the thought of quitting their nightly conversations.

As head chef, he was blessed to have a room of his own. He bounded up the stairs and closed the door. Inside, he removed his boots and tossed them into a corner, before falling backward across the bed. It wasn't until he made the decision to cut back on his time with Tabby, that Adam realized how lonely he really was. It would be worse now that he knew what her company meant to him. He had little in common with the rest of the kitchen staff. Soon, he would try to request time off to make a visit home. For his peace of mind, he needed to see his family.

7

Tabby sat on the swing hanging in the garden's gazebo and tucked her navy skirt under her legs. No longer feverish, she needed the fresh air, and the sun warming her shoulders felt wonderful. She had wanted to go to church, but the simple act of dressing had left her shaking. Most likely, she should have remained in bed. But birds sang outside her window, the sun woke her by kissing her cheeks, and Abigail's soft murmurs in her sleep had Tabby getting up to enjoy the day.

A breeze caressed her face as a sparrow chirped. After the rush of the previous month, a time of rest was exactly what Tabby needed. She laid her head against the wood slats and pushed the swing with her foot, dragging the toe of her shoe back and forth in the grass.

One month ago she had started work as a Harvey Girl. She still hadn't determined whether or not she liked the job. Before Miss O'Connor's confession yesterday, Tabby would have said a definite no. Now, she wasn't so sure. Having Miss O'Connor say Tabby was like her, sent fingers of dread down her back. Someday, Tabby might want a family of her own. Maybe.

Although she was skittish about men, she might be willing to take a chance on one, eventually, because she might want children. But if she were head waitress, she couldn't marry. No matter. Tabby had five months to decide whether she wanted to sign on for another six months. No one said she had to be a head waitress someday. Most likely, Tabby would stick with her original plan of moving down the line every six months, meeting new people, seeing new places. And she would try not to be lonely while she did.

A giggle came from the bushes behind her. Tabby stood. "Abigail?"

"Shhh." Abigail's head parted a juniper bush. Her hair flowed around her shoulders and the top button of her blouse had come undone. "We don't want to be caught."

Tabby put her hands on her hips. "Who are you with?"

"Josiah." Abigail slapped behind her. "Stop, I'm talking."

"Are you crazy?" Tabby shook her head. "Miss O'Connor will fire you for sure." The rules were stricter for immoral behavior with men than for merely talking to them. There would be no warning if Abigail and Josiah were found out. Miss O'Connor would fire her on the spot.

"Not if she doesn't catch me. Don't tell." Abigail winked and ducked out of sight.

Abigail might be the one Tabby considered a close friend, but she didn't agree with the girl's choices. Dawdling in the bushes with a man! As Abigail's closest friend at the restaurant, Tabby considered it her duty to have a serious discussion with the other girl about her wayward actions.

The afternoon's peacefulness shattered, Tabby headed to the kitchen to fix a light lunch. She nodded at the round, pleasant-faced woman who filled in for the rest of the kitchen staff on Sundays, and stepped into the coolness of the pantry.

Maybe she could eat a couple of slices of buttered toast. Something that wouldn't upset her stomach. Surely she could make toast. She hated asking the cook to make her something other than what the customers were eating. After all, the woman had more than enough work. While Tabby ate, she would try to figure out a way to keep her roommate from sabotaging her job.

She took the butter and headed out to the kitchen for bread. She took two slices from the mound on the counter then eyed the large stove.

"Need any help?" Adam snuck up behind her.

She gasped and whirled. "Don't do that. You scared five years off my life. I'm making toast, if you must know."

"Don't do a lot of cooking, do you?" He grinned and leaned against the counter, crossing his feet at the ankles.

"Of course I do."

"Then why not use the oven over there."

Tabby stomped her foot. "Oh, you." Must he play with her so?

"I'll do that for you, miss." The cook ambled up and took the bread from Tabby. "I don't like novices working with my stove, and it is Mr. Foster's day off."

"Thank you, but I don't want to bother you."

"Nonsense. Won't take me but a minute."

Tabby stepped back, needing space between herself and Adam. The scent of his shaving cream teased her senses and made her head whirl. Or maybe that was her cold. Nevertheless, she backed away.

"I'm glad you're feeling better." Adam stepped closer.

"Just tired." Tabby reached for a glass, anything to keep occupied. If she stared into his face, she would drown, not only in the flecks of gold in his blue eyes, but in the dimple in his right cheek as well. She didn't want to fall for him. They could be nothing but friends. A fine gentleman like him would want nothing to do with a girl like Tabitha. Nothing serious, anyway. "And hungry. I've not had breakfast."

"Neither have I. Maybe we should eat together."

Tabby closed her eyes and sighed. "It isn't allowed, and you know it."

"Where's the harm in two people sharing a corner of a big kitchen?" His eyes twinkled.

After Miss O'Connor's surprising confession that Tabby was one of her best girls, she didn't want anyone to jeopardize her future, not even Adam. Somehow she needed to squelch her growing attraction for him. After all, the man seemed to disregard the rules at every turn when it came to talking with her. Even if Tabby weren't bound by the restrictions of being a Harvey Girl, she doubted she would have much to do with a man who had such little regard for his employer's wishes. No, a man like that was too much like Pa. And Pa had spent more nights in jail than at home it seemed.

That wasn't fair, she chided herself. Adam didn't seem to be anything like Pa. The man just hovered over Tabby like a ray of sunshine, and she needed to put a stop to that real quick.

"I'll have my breakfast in my room," Tabby said, accepting her plate from the cook. "I should squeeze in a nap so I'm fit for work tomorrow."

"You aren't better?" He tried to touch her forehead.

"Adam, really." Tabby slapped his hand away. Must he be so forward? "I will see you tomorrow." With her nose in the air, she stormed past him. She'd been looking forward to a quiet afternoon in the garden, too. That man! Handsome or not, she didn't want him, or anyone else, to baby her so.

~

Adam's stomach dropped when Tabby said she needed to lie down. Should she be out of bed? Should he find Miss O'Connor? He ran his hands through his hair. What if Tabby were to fall ill and die as his wife had done? His knees threatened to give way.

"Are you all right, Mr. Foster?" The cook stared with compassionate eyes. "Not taking ill, too, are you?"

He waved off her concern. "No, just need some fresh air." He rushed out the back door and leaned against the building. He had done what he said he wouldn't ever do again. Come to care for a woman.

Well, he wouldn't allow it to grow. He could keep an eye on her from a distance. No more talks on the stoop. He plopped to the top step and put his head in his hands. Loneliness could be lived through. Losing another love could not. He pushed to his feet.

Who was he kidding? He could no more give up his so-called friendship with Tabby than he could rope the moon. He'd pray for her safety, watch her closely, and take her to California with him. She said she wanted adventure and travel instead of marriage, but maybe she would come around in time.

He hadn't watched Marilyn closely enough. He wouldn't make that mistake with Tabby.

Laughter drifted from the gazebo and Adam headed in that direction. Anything to pull him from his thoughts and solitude.

One of the waitresses emerged from the bushes and straightened her clothing. She giggled again and turned, fixing her hair as she did. Adam ducked around the corner of the building, wanting to avoid the awkwardness of discovering a forbidden tryst. Was there nowhere besides his room to spend a Sunday afternoon in peace?

He stared east, envisioning home. The family was most likely relaxing on the porch after stuffing themselves with Ma's Sunday roast. He remembered all the times with Marilyn by his side that the family had simply sat around and talked.

Tomorrow, Pa would be harvesting the fields, and Ma would be in the kitchen or doing laundry with his sister's help. Ma and Pa were getting too old for such hard work. At least when they had their own restaurant, Adam would take over the cooking duties, leaving Ma to do something less physical. Sometimes Adam wondered about the wisdom of leaving them to keep the farm going while he traveled the country to raise funds. Maybe if he'd stayed at home and helped, the land would be more productive.

The back door banged closed, and Tabby exited the building, her reticule slung over her arm. Without a glance his direction, she headed around the corner.

Adam followed, keeping a distance behind her as she took the walk alongside the railroad tracks and down Main Street. Most of the girls did their shopping on Sundays, since that was their only day off. The mercantile would open for them if the owners were around to hear the bell.

Tabby stopped in front of the store, pulled the rope that triggered the bell inside, then cupped her hands around her face and peered inside the window. After a few minutes, the door opened, and she disappeared inside.

Glad to see she apparently felt better, Adam sat on a bench to wait. Maybe she would need help carrying a package. If he were lucky, she would accept a lunch invitation. They could go to Betty's Boarding House and pretend there weren't silly rules hanging over their heads.

He leaped to his feet when Tabby stepped out, a wrapped package in her arms. Sitting on top was a box tied with a red and white checked ribbon. Adam grinned. She liked chocolates.

"Good afternoon." He jogged to her side.

She sighed. "Good afternoon, Adam."

"May I escort you to lunch later?" He felt like a young boy with his first crush. Nothing about the look on Tabby's face said she was happy to see him.

"I like you, Adam. I really do, but—" She took a deep breath. "I'm rethinking the wisdom of our friendship. I have no intentions of staying here. I told you on the train I want adventure."

"Have an ice cream with me."

"No."

"I'm only asking for friendship, Tabby."

Her gaze connected with his. "So you say, yet your actions prove otherwise."

"If I were one of the girls asking you for a treat, would you accept?"

She cocked her head. "Of course, but you aren't one of the girls. Keep it at our occasional evening conversations, please." She marched down the sidewalk.

Instead of following, he watched her go, her dark skirt swaying around her ankles. She might refuse his invitations, but she couldn't stop him from keeping an eye on her. Whistling, he headed in the opposite direction. At the first opportunity, he would go into the mercantile and purchase the biggest box of chocolates they carried.

At church that morning, the pastor had spoken about how God loved giving His children the desires of their hearts. Adam's desire lay in storefront property in San Francisco and in a girl with hair the color of sunshine. He prayed God would grant both desires. Self-promises or not, Adam knew he had lost his resolve when he sat down next to Tabby on that first train. He needed to find a way to get her to consider marriage to him and a life in San Francisco as a large enough adventure.

He laughed, remembering the confusion on her face when she eyed the stove that morning. It was a good thing he knew how to cook, because one way or the other, Tabby McClelland was going to San Francisco with him as his wife.

8

Tabby clutched her box of chocolates and yards of forest green wool. The wool was for a new skirt, but the chocolate she intended as a gift for Miss O'Connor. The woman might be lonely, what with being a head waitress for so many years. Most likely her loneliness made her crotchety, and nothing cheered a person like chocolate.

After the walk to town and back, not to mention rejecting Adam, Tabby's head and heart ached. First order of business for the afternoon would definitely be the planned nap and a conversation with God to take away the growing feelings she had for Adam.

Why did Adam insist on asking for more from her than friendship? Why couldn't men be happy with the small things? Pa's shenanigans were still too fresh in her mind, as was the memory of the wounded look in Mama's eyes. Tabby shook her head. She would have to know a man for many months before she would fully trust him, if then. He would need to have a thirst for adventure, which she was sure Adam had. But still, a mere thirty days of friendship did not give her peace in her heart.

Tabby stopped at the top of the stairs. Miss O'Connor stood facing into Abigail and Tabby's bedroom. Loud sobs came from inside.

"Quickly, Miss Smythe, I don't have all day."

"Please, Miss O'Connor, it won't happen again. This job is all I have."

Tabby moved closer, taking care not to clack her heels. She had no desire for the head waitress's wrath to turn her way because she made too much noise on the stairs.

"You should have thought of that before engaging in immoral acts." Miss O'Connor sniffed. "My girls are to exhibit the utmost decorum at all times. We have new girls arriving today, and what kind of example do you set? No, it is imperative that you leave. You and the young man can continue your behavior elsewhere. Scandalous, the way the two of you carried on...in public!" She looked over her shoulder at Tabby.

"Stop eavesdropping and help this wanton woman pack." With that, she spun on her heel and marched down the stairs.

"Here." Tabby rushed to Abigail's side. "I bought some chocolates. Sit and tell me what happened."

They perched on Abigail's bed, and Tabby unwrapped the box. Her roommate needed the candy more than Miss O'Connor.

"You saw Josiah and me. Well, when I entered the kitchen, Josiah ran up behind me and kissed my neck."

She grabbed a piece of candy. "Right in front of the wagon boss. Only we didn't know she was standing in the pantry. Evil witch, always spying."

Voicing her own opinion on Abigail's behavior wouldn't help so Tabby bit into a cream-filled bonbon and reined in her tongue. A burst of vanilla mixed with the chocolate tantalized her taste buds. They were worth the expense after all, especially when Abigail's tears stopped after her third piece.

"I didn't like this job anyway," she said. "Too hard. Josiah and I are going to go west where we'll work in a gambling hall and become richer than we ever dreamed."

Tabby stopped chewing for a moment, then swallowed. The large piece threatened to lodge in her throat, and she grabbed for a glass of water on the side table. How could she squash the silly girl's dreams, dreams that would only lead her to ruin? Abigail was heading to the same den of iniquity the pastor back home thought the Harvey restaurants were.

Tabby moved to the small window nestled between the beds and raised the window. She spotted a familiar figure running to the train station. "Are you sure that's what you want? Those places are dangerous, I've heard."

"They can't be that bad. Besides Josiah will marry me, and we'll be happy no matter where we are." Standing, Abigail grabbed a dress from a hook then shoved it into a satchel.

"The same Josiah who is getting on the train this very moment?" Tabby watched as without a backward glance, the young man grabbed a handrail and hoisted himself up the ramp.

Tabby faced a stunned Abigail. "I don't think the man plans on sticking around." Her gut clenched for the pain on her friend's face.

"He left me?" Abigail sank back to the bed and covered her face with her hands. "What am I going to do now?"

"Wait here." Tabby dashed out of the room and ran downstairs. She should have saved the candy. She could have used it to sweeten the head waitress's attitude.

She found Miss O'Connor in the kitchen. When Tabby entered, Adam turned his back to her, and the pale-faced head waitress stared with an unblinking gaze out the back door.

"Miss O'Connor." Tabby twisted her hands in her skirt.

The woman heaved a sigh. "Yes, Miss McClelland."

"I'm asking you to reconsider letting Abigail go." Please, have some mercy.

"Impossible." Miss O'Connor clamped her lips together.

"She has nowhere else to go. I saw Josiah boarding the train. Please, give her another chance." Tabby took a deep breath. "I will be personally responsible for her."

"Very well." Miss O'Conner waved a hand and strode for the door. "I'm too disheartened to care that one of my girls would behave in such a manner. Tell her to be at her station in the morning as usual."

Tabby clapped her hands together. "Thank you so much." She hefted her skirts and raced back to her room, her headache all but forgotten.

~

Adam slammed down the lid to the stew he was helping prepare for the Sunday cook. He didn't need to prepare meals on his day off, but usually the work relaxed him. Not today. Even after a rejuvenating Sunday morning at church, his nerves were strung tight. Now, he was short a helper again. All because somebody couldn't keep his hands off the girls. Adam shook his head, remembering Josiah's warnings about Tabby. The man should have heeded his own advice.

An advertisement in tomorrow's newspaper ought to round up help soon enough. Adam lowered the flame on the stove. His day had gone from pleasant to disappointing all within the space of an hour. Hopefully, Tabby would meet him on the stoop later that evening.

By the time the sun dropped behind the horizon, he couldn't wait to step outside. He hoped conversation with a pretty girl would chase away his rotten mood. Throwing a dishtowel on the counter, he shoved the back door open and stepped into a mild spring night.

A cloudless sky lit by thousands of diamond-like stars invited him to sit, lean back, and gaze at the night sky. A slight breeze carried the sweet aroma of honeysuckle. The squeak of the door, and a floral scent, alerted him to Tabby's presence. He smiled and kept staring at the sky. The rose water she wore brought back memories of Marilyn's lavender scent. He thanked God the women were different. It wouldn't do to start comparing them.

He didn't know how long they sat there, not speaking, only that he enjoyed every moment of sharing the heaven's wonders with her. Occasionally, she'd shift, bringing her arm into contact with his and sending tremors up his spine. After a while, she sighed and stood, then went back inside.

Why weren't they ever caught? Adam leaned forward, dangling his hands between his knees. They sat on the stoop most nights, in plain sight of anyone watching, yet no one said a word, other than Josiah. He glanced toward heaven. Was God protecting them from criticism? Was it part of His grand plan for him and Tabby to be in Kansas at the same time?

At the thought, Adam's fear of losing Tabby lessened a little. He would still watch her with an almost obsessive eye, he couldn't help it after his failure to keep his wife safe, but he would try to leave Tabby in God's hands. He really would. Even if it meant a daily struggle to hand God the reins.

~

Tabby watched through the door as Adam stood on the top step. She wanted to talk to him, hear his deep laugh, feel the playful bump of his shoulder when she said something silly, but after the way she brushed him off that afternoon, she didn't know how, and he seemed content to sit in silence.

When he turned to come back inside, she scampered out of sight and ran up the stairs. It had taken hours to calm Abigail after Josiah's desertion. The girl almost didn't accept the reinstatement of her job, saying there was nothing left for her here. Not until Tabby scared her with made up tales of California bordellos, did Abigail decide to stay. At least she thought they were made up stories. Having never been in one, but hearing plenty of tales, she did the best with what she had.

Relaxed after her quiet time with Adam, Tabby went to the parlor to browse for a book to read. She never did finish *Jane Eyre*. She ran her finger along the spines of the books. A shadow fell across the doorway. She knew without turning that Adam watched her.

What prompted him to care so much for a woman he had so recently met? Sometimes, a haunted look crossed his handsome features. One day, she would ask him what pained him from his past. By the time she held the book she sought, Adam was gone.

She was a foolish girl, dwelling on things that couldn't be, not if she wanted to fulfill her dreams. Book in hand, she moved back to her room where Abigail sat in front of their shared mirror, running a brush through her blond tresses.

"Thank you for saving my job." Abigail sniffed, never stopping the long strokes of the brush. "I didn't deserve it."

"I hope you learned a lesson." Tabby set her book on the small table beside her bed. "Josiah's cowardly dash away reconfirmed my lack of faith in men. Most men are scoundrels and not to be trusted. A girl needs to learn to rely on herself and God."

Abigail turned. "I didn't know you hated men."

"I don't hate men. I just don't have time for them. In a man's mind, women are nothing but property to be owned. Something to use and throw away." Tabby reached behind to unfasten her dress. Her words sounded harsh, even to her ears. Choking back sobs of her own, she inhaled sharply. She wouldn't cry. Her views had been formed years ago. She couldn't change them now.

"I thought you had something with the chef." Abigail's brow furrowed.

"We're only friends."

A small smile crossed Abigail's sad face. "Women and men can't be friends. Especially when the man looks like our chef." She waved her brush at Tabby. "You think no one knows of your visits on the back stoop, but they do. Watch yourself, my friend. You don't want to be in my shoes.

"One of the new gals said it isn't against the rules to keep company with men, only to keep company without a chaperone. That's what the parlor is for. The 'courting parlor' they call it. Be careful. Miss O'Connor is tougher than some of the other wagon bosses, I've heard, and much more strict."

Tabby wouldn't need to worry about impropriety. Nothing in heaven or on earth could weaken her resolve.

9

Tabby took her place beside the coffee carafes, happy for her new and easier job as a drink girl, and watched Miss O'Connor meet the new arrivals. The head waitress informed her that morning that she would remain in Topeka, but would have a new roommate. Abigail was being sent to a restaurant in New Mexico.

As much as Tabby would have liked to move on in her quest for adventure, she vowed to be content where she was. For now. She loved her job and the skills she learned each day. Skills that would serve her well when she finally settled with a family of her own, should she decide on that way of life. Never before had she had the chance to make people as happy as the Harvey customers were when they finished their meals. The smiles on their faces and the thank you's from their lips gave Tabby great satisfaction in a job well done.

"I've heard great things about you, Miss

McClelland." The restaurant manager, Mr. Hastings sidled up next to her. The scent of his hair pomade threatened to close Tabby's lungs. "I was very glad to hear you weren't moving on. Each day is much more enjoyable when surrounded by beauty such as yours."

The man's lecherous smile made her skin crawl. "Thank you, sir. I do my best to perform my duties proficiently."

He nodded. "I also heard that Miss O'Connor set your points down to ten. Maybe I could put a good word in with Mr. Harvey when he visits next month. That ought to take your number down still further." He trailed a finger down her arm, burning through the cotton of her blouse.

Tabby stiffened and took a step away. "And what would I have to give you in return, Mr. Hastings?" *Hold your tongue, remain respectful.* She had heard rumors of what some girls did to gain status, things she would never contemplate. Still, it would do her no good to rile the manager.

"I'm sure we could come up with something beneficial to us both." He patted her folded hands and moved to where Miss O'Connor waited.

When donkeys wore lace-up boots! Tabby shuddered. The nerve of the man. Not only had the rumors of his advances toward the other waitresses reached her ears, but tales of many clandestine rendezvous with Miss O'Conner had also. Of course, Tabby wasn't one to listen to rumors, but the manager's forward actions with her led her to believe that at least some of the tales were true. Did the man have no shame?

Obviously Mr. Harvey had no idea what type of man

he had hired as manager. Well, things always had a way of coming to the surface. She would leave Mr. Hastings to God and Mr. Harvey.

She refused to dwell on such unpleasantness. Instead, she focused on providing the exemplary service the Harvey restaurants were famous for. Whether some people chose to engage in certain activities need not concern her. Still, she would steer clear of Mr. Hastings.

Two new girls, escorted by Miss O'Connor, moved through the restaurant. Had Tabby looked that confused and nervous on her first day? She smiled a greeting as they sailed past her and prepared for the breakfast rush.

"I'm leaving on this train." She hadn't heard Abigail come up beside her. "I guess it's for the best. I still have a job, and Miss O'Connor doesn't have to look at me."

Tabby wrapped her arms around her friend. "I will miss you. Please tell me you've learned from this experience."

"I have, and I've already said my goodbyes to Ingrid." Abigail hefted her bag. "On to better things, right? We can keep in touch by letter." Tears shimmered in her eyes. "I hope your new roommate realizes what a treasure you are."

Tabby choked back tears. "God go with you, my friend. I wish I had more chocolates to send with you."

"Me too." Abigail took a deep breath and marched out the door.

Tabby's breath shuddered at the loss of her good friend. Life awarded so few of them, especially for the daughter of a drunken womanizer. Growing up, most of her classmates' parents forbade their children to play with her. Her family wasn't considered good enough with their ramshackle house and hand-me-down clothes. Abigail might not have always been morally correct in her actions, but Tabby had learned to look at a person's heart. Abigail had a good one underneath her flirtation manner.

She got a glimpse of Adam as he exited the kitchen with a platter of ham, and she averted her gaze. With Abigail's departure, it became even more imperative that she avoid Adam. It was better for both of them. Although she didn't think she would mind being shuttled off to another restaurant, she didn't want it to be under unpleasant circumstances.

As the now familiar sounds of train passengers eating breakfast and the aromas from the kitchen swirled around her, Tabby filled a wheeled tray with coffee, tea, water, and milk. Drinks at the ready, she moved around the room filling customer's mugs and glasses.

Which one of the new girls would share a room with her? The tall, raven-haired girl or the one with hair the color of chestnuts? Tabby prayed the girl would be kind and friendly. With her uncertain feelings for Adam, and the stress of trying to excel as a Harvey Girl, she didn't welcome more tension in her life.

"Is it possible to have coffee and water?" A man wearing a business suit held up his mug.

"Why, yes sir." Tabby filled his mug and smiled. "You may have coffee, tea, milk, and water, if you prefer."

He laughed. "You're a cheeky thing. Are you on that list of items a man can have?"

"You can only dream so, sir." Keeping the smile on her face, she moved on to the next customer, the man's chuckles following her. She didn't mind a little harmless teasing. After all, she could give back what she received. No, she didn't care for the men who wanted to grab her or got angry at her negative responses. Those were the men that bothered her.

Mr. Hastings grinned as he stood outside the door to the kitchen. Tabby almost hoped someone would barge through the swinging doors and hit him upside the head. Anything to wipe away the leer on his face.

~

Adam wanted to punch his boss in the face. Only a blind man wouldn't see the looks the man gave Tabby. Almost as if he could see her unclothed. Adam punched the bread dough, envisioning the lump as Mr. Hastings face.

Dough pounded, he placed a clean towel over it and moved on to cleaning the dishes from breakfast. He scraped soap into the washbasin. *Please, God, let someone responsible answer the advertisement.* He couldn't continue cooking and doing the cleanup too.

Miss O'Connor led two new girls into the kitchen. "This is our chef, Mr. Foster. Once you've tasted his culinary delights, I'm sure you'll agree we have hired the best."

A tall dark-haired beauty batted her eyelashes and dipped her head in a coy manner. She didn't fool Adam a bit. He'd seen husband hunters before. She would be as tenacious as a hound dog on a scent to achieve that goal. Well, she could go look somewhere else.

Dishes piled on the counter to dry, Adam sliced the ham and beef for lunch. If someone didn't respond to his advertisement, he might have to ask for a couple of waitresses to help. If given the chance, he'd request Tabby. Of course, now that she was a drink girl, he didn't worry as much about her working too hard. What would it be like to work side-by-side with her, engaging in conversation and honest teasing?

He stopped and glanced out the window. The late morning sun cast the gazebo and trees into shadow and beckoned Adam to enjoy the warmth of a summer morning. He definitely needed a vacation. A couple of days to head home and check on the family would suffice.

Soon, fragrant heaps of meat for sandwiches or platters sat on gleaming silver trays. Adam arched his back, popping the kinks from his spine. If he hurried, he would have time for his own lunch before the customers arrived. He made two ham sandwiches and set one aside.

The swinging doors opened and Tabby wheeled in the drink cart. "Goodness, folks are thirsty." She swiped the back of her hand across her forehead.

"I made you a sandwich." Adam handed her the extra one.

She eyed the plate in his hand and sighed before accepting. "Thank you." She perched on a stool next to the counter. "You really are a persistent man, Adam Foster."

"Yes, I am." He bit into his lunch. Should he let her know that he would warn Mr. Hastings away from her if she wished? Or wait and see whether she would ask for his help?

Her chocolate-colored eyes peered over the sandwich. A shuttered look crossed them before her lids dropped, and she paid an undue amount of attention to her food. He grinned and enjoyed the blush spreading across her cheeks, content to eat in silence if that guaranteed him her company.

"That was delicious. Thank you." She hopped from the stool, brushed crumbs from her skirt, and skedaddled out the door as if she'd seen another mouse.

Adam laughed. She could pretend she didn't feel anything for him, but it was nothing more than an act.

~

Tabby dashed down the path to the gazebo. Why must Adam stare at her so intently? She couldn't think when his gaze burned her the way it did.

Short of breath, face flushed, she plopped onto the swing. Maybe she could spare five minutes to sit and rock, a little time to gather her thoughts. She stilled as Miss O'Connor and the new waitresses peered out the upstairs window.

What kind of example did Tabby set, lounging in the sun, while work waited? She got to her feet and shuffled back to the restaurant to refill the drink pitchers.

In the kitchen, Mr. Hastings spoke with Adam about the evening's menu. Praying the man would leave her alone, Tabby moved past them, and grabbed fresh pitchers of milk from the cooled section of the pantry. When he turned and fixed his gaze on her, she rushed to the coffee pots. Staying busy would make it harder for him to speak with her. She hoped.

"Miss McClelland." Tabby turned at Miss O'Connor's greeting.

"Your roommate is Miss Merrilee Ramsey. I'm sure you two will become fast friends. There's enough time before lunch for you to show her where she'll be sleeping." Miss O'Connor lifted her chin.

"Yes, ma'am." Tabby smiled. Merrilee was the

darker-haired beauty.

Her new roommate turned a smile on Tabby that didn't quite reach her almost black eyes. "We're sure to become close." Her southern drawl almost sounded like a foreign language. She leaned in and whispered, "But not as close as I'd like to get to that handsome chef."

10

"Where are you going? It's Sunday morning." Merrilee sat up in bed, her face framed by the ruffle around the neckline of her nightgown.

"Church." Tabby poked the last pin in her hair. "I've stayed away too long." And been too lax on her Bible reading.

"The Bible is nothing but a book of fairy tales for weak minded people." Merrilee burrowed back under her blankets. "Besides, going to church seriously interferes with a girl's beauty sleep. My day will be better spent on sidling up to that handsome chef. He's been too busy all week to give me more than a passing glance."

Tabby rolled her eyes. Her roommate spent so much time on pursuits of beauty and even more talking about 'the handsome chef' until Tabby wanted to throw a hairbrush at her. Tabby slipped her reticule over her arm. "I'll see you later. Enjoy your rest."

Handsome chef, indeed. Tabby spotted Adam strolling down the street toward church. She grinned, suffering only a moment of conviction at being happy to know that.Merrilee would have to wait until later to spend time with the object of her affection. She tried to be friendly with her roommate, but the girl's high-handed manner grated on Tabby's nerves.

Increasing her pace, Tabby hurried to the church steps, and dashed inside as the bells tolled. She chose a seat toward the back and kept herself from glancing around to locate Adam, not wanting the distraction of having him within easy sight. Today was the Lord's day, and she wanted to concentrate on the worship and the teaching, not wondering where her friendship with Adam might be heading.

Later, she looked forward to a simple afternoon on the gazebo swing, book in hand, and a glass of tea close by.

'Rock of Ages' soon rang through the church. Tabby sang along with the congregation and let God's love fill her. A rich baritone behind her caused her to glance over her shoulder. Adam winked. Obviously the man had a talent for singing. She lowered her off-key voice and listened.

After they finished singing the morning hymns, Tabby's spirit rested. She settled back on the pew, eager to hear what the pastor had to say. An older gentleman, silver-haired and sharp-eyed, approached the simple wood podium.

"I am your temporary pastor, Nathaniel Harper, and I am blessed to be assigned to this wonderful congregation, if only for a short time." His gaze scanned the crowd. "Although, I must confess to being dismayed at discovering a Harvey restaurant in the lovely city of Topeka. A restaurant that actually trains our young women to be Harvey Girls."

Oh, no. Tabby slouched. A pastor with the same mindset as the one in St. Louis.

"Now, fellow parishioners, don't get me wrong, I'm sure not all the women employed at these restaurants are wanton women looking for an easy means of finding a husband. No sirree! Some are simply misguided young ladies, lured into a life of servitude to strange men. Women are not to work outside the home, other than to teach our young or to minister at church. Why, the very thought of them serving a man other than their husband is a travesty."

The pastor couldn't be serious. Tabby clutched her purse. Women worked in many fields, even as doctors. Had the man been living under a rock?

Could she skulk out without anyone noticing? She glanced over her shoulder. Adam caught her eye and winked. She forced a smile and returned her attention to the pastor. It wouldn't do to be caught sharing looks with a man, obviously. Not under the hawkeyed watch of Pastor Harper and especially not with both of them working at the Harvey restaurant.

Oh, she so wanted, no needed, to be filled and refreshed by God's Word. Instead, she had to listen to a man try to convince the citizens of Topeka that the Harvey Girls were wayward women.

She straightened. The anointed words of the hymns would carry her through the week, despite the pastor's opinion of her job. The man was wrong about the Harvey Girls, something he would realize once he came into the restaurant for a meal. Tabby vowed to be so kind and sweet the man would have to change his outlook.

"So as we conclude today's message on temptation..."

Tabby jerked her attention back to the front of the church. Had he actually given a sermon and she'd missed it?

"Go with God's grace that you may resist the devil."

The devil in the black and white uniform of a Harvey Girl, no doubt. Tabby jumped to her feet and rushed out the door before the tears stinging her eyes escaped.

"Tabby." Adam trotted to her side. "I'd be pleased if you would accompany me to lunch."

"Aren't you afraid of being around such an evil temptress?" She whirled, clutching her Bible to her chest.

He took a step back. "Don't let the words of small-minded people affect you."

"It's too late. I'm already burned." How would the pastor treat her once he discovered she was one of the infamous Harvey girls? Would he put a scarlet H on her chest and run her out of town?

"I'm sure most of the townspeople don't share his views."

She shrugged. "Maybe." The restaurant did do a booming business every day. Surely folks wouldn't be quick to order a meal from a disreputable place.

"About my lunch invitation?"

"I'm sorry, but it seems my appetite has fled." She resumed her march toward the restaurant. "Besides, if we were seen together, it would only convince Pastor Harper that his misguided notion is correct. Good afternoon, Adam."

By the time she reached her room, her temper had come to a full boil. She thanked God the room was empty. Most likely Merrilee lay in wait somewhere, ready to set her snare for Adam. She'd be more than happy to accept a lunch invitation with him with no regard to the consequences.

Tabby tossed her purse on the bureau then plopped across the bed. Tears ran down her cheeks, soaking her pillow. She palmed them away. How she'd looked forward to finally going to church. Thank goodness Pastor Harper was temporary, but how long would he be in Topeka? And would he affect her job?

"He's back." Merrilee danced into the room. "He's in the parlor reading the newspaper." She clasped her hands to her bosom. "I have the sudden urge to read."

Why bother coming in to tell me? The woman seemed determined to be a thorn in her side. What did she care? She had no claim on him other than friendship. "Have fun."

"You'll never catch a man if you keep such a sour attitude." Merrilee stepped in front of the mirror and pinched her cheeks, bringing a touch of red to her porcelain skin.

"Who said I was looking for one?" Tabby heaved a sigh and sat up.

"Why ever not?" The other girl turned, her brow furrowed. "That's the whole reason I left Savannah."

Tabby sighed. The girl obviously wanted to share her life story. Why couldn't she leave her to wallow in self-pity? "How so?"

"During the war, my family lost their fortune, and Mama said being a Harvey Girl would bring a parade of worthy husbands past me."

"I don't think chefs make a lot of money." Would the woman ever leave her in peace? She didn't care about Merrilee's prospects for finding a husband. More important things occupied her mind.

"He's not a husband prospect, silly girl. He's just someone to play with until a rich man comes along."

Tabby hid her clenched fists in the folds of her skirt.

~

Adam peered over the top of his paper as one of the new waitresses, Merrilee he thought her name was, sashayed in and headed straight for the small bookshelf which housed approximately twenty novels. He raised the paper. She didn't strike him as the reading type. He winced, needing to repent of his unfair labeling. He knew better than to judge a person by her looks. Perhaps a woman thirsty for knowledge hid behind the simpering smile and southern cooing.

"Ahem." A few seconds passed. "Ahem."

Ignoring the not-so-subtle attempts at getting his attention wasn't working. Adam lowered the newspaper. "May I help you?"

Merrilee laid her index finger across her lips. "I'm looking for a book to read, but must say I haven't the faintest idea which one."

"What do you like to read?" Adam folded the paper and stood.

"Romance." She fluttered her lashes.

Adam's mouth dried. "I'm afraid I can't help you there." Very few of the girls frequented the parlor, preferring instead to spend their few precious moments off work in their rooms. He'd thought he could enjoy a couple of hours of solitude. No wonder Tabby fled to the gazebo at every opportunity. He'd almost followed, but sensed she wanted to be alone. Now, he was stuck with a woman who eyed him like a hungry cat after a mouse.

"Surely a learned man such as yourself can help a girl with some romance?" Merrilee swished her skirts and moved closer. "My name is Merrilee."

"Mine's Adam. Sorry, I don't read novels." Tucking his newspaper under his arm, he squeezed past her and dashed out the door. That was a close call. The last thing he wanted was to be trapped by a man-hungry woman whose daddy probably had a big shotgun.

He paused on the path leading to the gazebo. Tabby bent over a book, her blond hair shining in the afternoon sun. He wanted to join her, but feared rejection. Nightly visits on the back stoop were rare now. Tabby almost acted as if she were afraid of something. Of him. He was lucky if she showed up three nights out of the week.

He headed for the woods at the edge of town. It was a serene place with a small brook babbling over rocks. He thought of Tabby. There had to be a way to spend more time with her. At first, he had hoped they could get involved at church, but after today's sermon, that wasn't an option. At least not until a new pastor arrived.

A boulder sat beside the creek, its height perfect as a backrest. Adam lowered himself to the soft ground and shook his paper open. The great outdoors, something to read, birds singing, all provided the perfect Sunday afternoon. All he lacked was a pretty girl to share the day with.

Leaves rustled along the path and Adam straightened. Seconds later, the hem of a blue cotton skirt came into view as if his thoughts had brought forth the very woman he wished to see. He smiled and raised his paper. Let Tabby say the first word.

She perched on the boulder. "Do you think the pastor is correct in his assumptions?"

Not the question Adam expected. He lowered the paper. "Not in the least." He faced her. "Sure, there are gals like Abigail who push the system, but most of the girls are upstanding, moral women. Like you, they are only women looking for a job."

"Am I moral?" She lifted her face to the sun. "Sometimes I feel my bitterness over my father rules every decision I make. That must grieve God terribly."

"What happened with your father?" When she didn't answer right away, Adam thought maybe she wouldn't.

She gave a sigh heavy enough to sink a ship. "Ma wasn't enough for him. Every night he came home smelling of liquor and cheap scent. I watched as Ma withered away. I realized true love rarely existed anymore, if it ever had." She slid from the boulder. "When I was a child, I believed in fairy tales, but no more."

Adam let his paper fall. He got to his feet, and took her hands. His thumbs caressed the rose petal softness. His large hands engulfed her small ones, filling him with an overwhelming need to protect her. Not that he didn't already feel that way, but having her close, hearing her vulnerability, made him want to grab her close and take her to a place where the world could no longer hurt her.

~

Tears stung Tabby's eyes. A lump grew in her throat. How long since someone had held her hands with tenderness? Not since Ma died. Pa hadn't shown her much physical affection at all that she could remember.

"I wish I could take away your pain." Adam's whisper floated over her like a soothing balm. "I can't, but our father in heaven can replace even the worst of earthly ones."

He held her hands tight.

She stiffened and tried to pull away. "I know that, but I don't need platitudes right now."

"And I don't mean to give them. I'm only trying to comfort you." He pulled her closer. "Let me."

A rock took up residence in her stomach. She couldn't allow herself to care for him as more than a friend. That could lead to heartache.

She shook her head. "I need to get back before we're discovered."

"Not yet. Please." He lowered his head and placed his lips on hers.

His kiss was tender, his lips soft but firm. Shivers raced up and down her spine. Her breathing stopped. Her heart raced. She leaned into his kiss, drawing on the affection he wanted to offer, then pulled away. "We can't do this, Adam. I'm not ready to put my heart at risk. I'm not sure if I ever will be. I'm sorry."

Gathering her skirt in her hands, she scrambled from the rock and sprinted for the safety of her room.

Why couldn't she accept what Adam wanted to offer? Adam wasn't her father. Instead, he was a godly man who desired her company. But only because he didn't know the truth about Tabby's upbringing. He didn't know that her father was a drunk and a gambler.

Her tears had escalated to a full sob fest by the time she reached her room and threw herself face down on the bed. Why did Adam have to kiss her? Now, he'd jeopardized their friendship. Even casual conversations would feel stilted. It couldn't change how she felt about marriage, nor about her longing for the adventure she'd craved since childhood.

Giving into childish emotion, she kicked and pounded the mattress. Instead of the peaceful Sunday she'd envisioned, it couldn't be more horrible.

Except for the kiss. She didn't know how to feel about Adam's lips on hers. She rolled to her back and smoothed a finger across her lips.

Merrilee marched into the room and approached the bed. She crossed her arms. "I'm telling Miss O'Connor that you were kissing the chef in the woods."

11

Tabby woke the next morning achy and with eyes as dry as the desert. After trying to convince Merrilee not to run to the head waitress, she had tossed and turned all night. Not until she promised to stay away from Adam so Merrilee could get close to him, did the other woman finally go to bed.

Now, a day of dragging feet loomed ahead of her. She groaned and rolled from bed and stared at Merrilee's empty bed. If Tabby didn't want to be overshadowed by the new girl's desire to shine, she would need to move faster and work harder.

The cool boards under her feet as she shuffled to the mirror signified that summer was drawing to a close. Tabby ran her fingers over the monogram of a flower on her mother's hairbrush. What would she have thought of her daughter becoming a Harvey Girl? She would be pleased, no doubt, that Tabby got away from the difficulties of her childhood.

The poverty and hand-me-down clothes. Rented rooms in buildings with more rats than people. Tabby's job allowed her independence, a good salary, and the chance to improve herself. There wasn't a lot more a girl could do for herself, other than find an upstanding, godly man to share her life with.

She pulled her brush through her hair with long rough strokes. First the church service yesterday, then Adam's kiss, and finally Merrilee's threats. The last month had brought her nothing but chaos. Her hand stilled, and she laughed. Well, she said she wanted adventure. It seemed like she'd found it. She'd also found a Godly man, if only she could let go of her fears and welcome his affections. Why couldn't she?

Because Tabby had no idea what love was. She couldn't use her parents as an example. Maybe Adam occupied so much of her thoughts because he was a large part of her excitement of being in a new place with a promising career. That must be it. Adam was a symbol of security, something Tabby's life had always lacked.

As long as she remembered the reason her heart leaped at the sight of him, the fact being what he represented, more than anything romantic, she could do her job effectively and look forward to more adventures.

Her steps lighter despite her lack of sleep, Tabby dressed and headed downstairs to begin her work day.

A frowning Miss O'Connor met her at the restaurant entrance. "I'm sorry to say I need to temporarily revoke your privilege of being the drink girl."

Merrilee must have told her about Adam! Tabby

decided to feign innocence. "Did I do something wrong?"

"No." Miss O'Connor waved a hand. "On the contrary. It seems Ingrid decided to run off with a man last night and now we are short a trainer. There is no one more qualified than you to fill that position."

Another waitress lost? Did these young women not realize that by running off while under contract they were behaving exactly as Pastor Harper said they would? Tabby expelled the breath she'd been holding. "Yes, ma'am. Wherever you need me."

Miss O'Connor turned and stared out the window. "Do you know why the girls seem so unhappy under my rule?" She glanced over her shoulder. "You may be honest."

"You have a tendency to be rather harsh." Tabby clapped a hand over her mouth. Why couldn't she think before speaking?

"Don't fret." Miss O'Connor breathed deeply through her nose. "I admit maybe I'm too hard on the girls. Perhaps I should be more nurturing, more open to them coming to me with their problems. More like a mother figure than the wagon boss they call me." She quirked her right eyebrow. "All I'm asking is that they be discreet, as you are in your dealings with Mr. Foster." The corner of her mouth lifted. "Yes, I'm aware of your back stoop conversations, and since no one has complained about a lack of decorum on your part, I've chosen not to say anything. You have proven to be an upstanding example of a Harvey employee."

"Thank you." Tabby really couldn't figure out the head waitress. Either she was blunt to the point of rudeness or friendly. "Most of the girls seem quite happy in their jobs. Maybe the choices of a few have nothing to do with your leadership."

"Perhaps. My job is a lonely one, as you will, no doubt, figure out for yourself someday. But it also has its rewards." She blinked wet eyes, her lashes fluttering like the wings of a mockingbird, before she marched into the restaurant.

Tabby planted her fists on her hips. Now, that was a cry for friendship or her name wasn't Tabitha McClelland. She'd purchase another box of chocolates at the first opportunity. Maybe she and Miss O'Connor could share them as she and Abigail had.

The conversation made Tabby all the more determined not to settle in one place. Sure, she might be lonely moving down the line, but think of the people she would meet, the folks she could cheer with a friendly smile and good food. Not staying put lessened people's ability to hurt her, shatter her emotions, or keep her from her dream.

Tiredness forgotten, Tabby tightened the bow on her starched apron and pushed through the restaurant doors. Her heart fell at the sight of the girl waiting for her. Merrilee had to be the worst person she could have thrust upon her to train. The other girl didn't look any happier.

Merrilee's dark eyes narrowed, and she turned away. Tabby waited for her to renege on her promise not to say anything about Adam. When she didn't, Tabby's heart lifted from the pit of her stomach. She could do this, even if Merrilee's response felt like a frigid winter wind.

"Good morning." Adam bent close to her ear, sending goose bumps down her arms, before he moved past, his arms full of fresh bread.

"Good morning." Tabby grinned. Now that Miss O'Connor knew of the innocent time she spent with Adam, she no longer had anything to fear from the irate woman who stood next to her. No, all Tabby had to fear was her own growing attraction to a man who clearly wanted to settle down and have a family.

Merrilee bumped her shoulder, knocking her back a step, then batted her eyelashes at Adam. "Aren't you going to say good morning to me?" She pouted.

"Good morning to you." Adam gave her a nod and set the bread in a basket on the counter. "Best get busy, ladies. Train will be here soon."

"A scowl causes wrinkles. Please try a smile instead, Miss Ramsey. It's more attractive." Miss O'Connor sailed past them.

Tabby stifled a giggle. "We serve the tables over here." She led Merrilee to the tables overlooking the train platform. "When you take the drink order, you place the cups in the proper position so the drink girl knows exactly what the customer requested without having to ask." She pointed to a pad of paper in Merrilee's pocket.

"Feel free to write down the orders at first, but train yourself to remember what the customer wants. And always treat the customer as if they are the best thing you've seen all day."

"You're enjoying this, aren't you?" Merrilee crossed her arms. "Having to train me? Well, I'll be requesting a new trainer at the first opportunity. And don't think you can give those simpering smiles to Adam without me telling the wagon boss. The sour old cow, telling me to smile."

Tabby raised her eyebrows. "Such venom from a southern lady. You may tell Miss O'Connor anything you desire. She already knows about me keeping company with Adam, and has no problem with the fact." With that, Tabby pasted on a smile and straightened as the morning train pulled into the station.

The other girl's gasp gave her great satisfaction. She knew she shouldn't behave so, but Merrilee did rile her to distraction. She'd try to behave better. Tomorrow. Today, she wouldn't let some Jezebel toy with Adam's affections. Not if she could help it.

She whispered a prayer of repentance. Adam was a full grown man capable of watching out for himself. After all, Merrilee definitely stated she wasn't looking for marriage unless a man had a lot of money. Tabby clenched her fists in the pockets of her apron. What if Adam were drawn in by her feminine wiles? Why should Tabby care? After all, they were nothing more than friends.

Then why did the thought of him with someone else feel like a dagger to her heart?

~

The new girl's attempts to engage Adam in conversation didn't escape him. Not that she wasn't lovely, but she didn't interest him. Not like Tabby. He much preferred feistiness to simpering eyelash batting, and the woman's obvious attempts at flirtation were annoying rather than charming.

He dumped flour into a bowl then added shortening. Busy chatter from the five new kitchen helpers, two boys and three young girls, brightened his heart. After half a year, the Topeka restaurant was booming, and he'd heard of more Harvey restaurants opening all the time.

Too many. His hands stilled. The more restaurants that opened, the more chance there was of Tabby moving on.

Mr. Hastings stepped into the kitchen. "Get a move on, folks. Train is here." He stepped to Adam's side. "I've also put a pistol under the lunch counter. Make sure the ladies know it's there."

"Why?" Adam stiffened.

"To discourage unwanted suitors, of course." Mr. Hastings smirked. "A tale came down the line of one of the customers assaulting one of the girls because his soup was cold." He patted Adam's shoulder. "It's just a precaution. Miss O'Connor will inform the rest of the staff. I presume you can shoot?"

"I'm a very good shot." Adam went back to his biscuit preparations. A gun. He shook his head. Not a good idea in his opinion. What if one of the girls got hold of the thing having no idea how to handle a weapon? Sure, most girls probably knew how to handle a pistol, but there were bound to be a few who didn't.

Tabby darted into the room and grabbed a basket of wrapped silverware. "Restaurant's full. It's going to be a busy day." She whirled to leave.

"Wait," he called before she could dash away.

She paused and raised her eyebrows in question.

"There's a gun behind the lunch counter," he whispered.

"I know. It's under the napkins."

"Do you know how to handle one?"

"Of course." She grinned and hurried out of the room.

Adam shook his head. Every day she amazed him.

He vowed to find out more about his reluctant friend.

No mention had been made about his stolen kiss. The way she'd raced away led him to believe the act hadn't pleased her, yet she didn't shun him. Although he had hope, he figured it best not to try again for a good long while. Only thing was, he didn't know how long he had before she left Topeka.

Biscuits mixed and cut, he slid them into the oven, then wiped his hands on a clean dishtowel. "All right, folks. The day gets busier from here. Dishes need to be kept clean and the food trays filled, especially behind the lunch counter. Folks don't have a lot of time to eat and don't need to be waiting for us."

The helpers scattered to their respective jobs as if he'd fired the beginning shot of a horse race.

"Telegram, Foster." Mr. Hastings barged into the kitchen, shoved the slip of paper into Adam's hands, then raced back to the dining room.

Adam scanned the notice. His heart stopped, and he sagged against the counter, reading the message again.

"Mother ill. Stop. Come home. Stop. Daphne."

12

Adam dashed upstairs and packed his bag. He couldn't get home soon enough. Hastings hadn't argued when Adam told him he needed to leave immediately because of a family emergency.

The next train left the station in less than half an hour. He at least needed a moment to say goodbye to Tabby.

He grabbed a few belongings and stuffed them in his bag, then he rushed to the dining room. He might be anxious about his mother, but missing Tabby pulled at his heart, too. What if she left while he was gone? His heart threatened to burst from his chest, not only from his rush in preparing to leave, but because of a flood of emotion. He spotted her at a table by the restaurant window. "Tabby."

She murmured something to Merrilee, before striding his way. "What's wrong? She laid a hand on his arm.

"You look upset."

He handed her the telegram. Her face paled as she read it. Closing her eyes, she handed the slip of paper back. "I'll pray for you and your mother."

"Won't you miss me?" *Please, say you will.*

Her eyes snapped open. "Of course I will." She raised her hand to his face, then dropped it before making contact. "We're the best of friends after all." Her chin quivered, and she looked away. But not before he saw the shimmer of tears in her eyes. Dare he hope she cried because he was leaving?

Stubborn woman. Couldn't she let him know that she would miss him desperately? Or was that only his wishful thinking? Why wouldn't she admit she had feelings for him? "Yeah, friends." He wanted to kiss her goodbye and show her exactly what he thought of their just being friends. Instead, he nodded and sprinted for the train.

While his thoughts were on his family, a piece of his heart remained in the restaurant with Tabby. If only she was here beside him. Her small smooth hand engulfed in his. Without a doubt, her presence would give him comfort.

He found a seat and plopped onto it, prepared to spend the ride staring out the window, worrying over Ma, and wondering about Tabby's feelings.

~

People didn't send telegrams unless the situation was dire.

Tabby moved back to her place where she could keep a watchful eye on Merrilee as the girl waited on customers. She lifted a prayer for the safety of Adam's mother and his quick return, shoving to the back of her mind how much she would miss him.

Dragging her attention back to her job, her gaze fell on Merrilee. Tabby was content with the knowledge that the woman couldn't snare Adam's affections while he was gone. Merrilee caught on quick to the art of serving people with efficiency and a smile. Almost as if she weren't the southern belle she pretended to be, but someone used to waiting on others. Tabby narrowed her eyes. There might be more to the woman than she'd first thought. Maybe she held a secret, waiting to be discovered.

Mr. Hastings stopped beside Tabby. "I'm going to find a temporary chef. Hopefully Mrs. Mayer can fill in on a more permanent basis than just Sundays." He leaned closer, his mouth inches from her ear. "Would you like to accompany me? I'm confident the restaurant can do without your services for an hour or two."

Tabby froze. Was he suggesting what she thought he suggested? After all, contacting their Sunday chef to fill in during Adam's absence wouldn't require a lot of time. No more than fifteen minutes or so. Planting her fists on her hips, she stepped back. "You, sir, are overstepping your boundaries. If you don't wish for the heel of my boot on your foot, I suggest you change your way of thinking." With that, she whirled and stomped to the kitchen.

How would she manage without her champion? Adam was the one person she could go to when she needed to vent her frustrations. He would listen, sometimes offering wise counsel. With Abigail also gone, she had no one. She couldn't go to Miss O'Connor, especially not with the rumors floating around about her and the manager. There was no one to tell about Mr. Hastings's lecherous comments or inappropriate actions.

Tabby kicked the garbage pail as she passed, ignoring the stunned looks on the faces of the kitchen help, and watched with satisfaction as the can wobbled, then righted itself. Continuing her temper tantrum, she marched outside and glared at the tree line. She envisioned Adam kissing her, and in her mind, she threw caution to the wind and returned his kiss with all the emotion she had in her. The type of kiss a woman gave the man she loved.

Would the world end if she gave in and welcomed his attention? Allowed him to court her? He seemed as far from Pa in his way of acting as the Atlantic Ocean was to the Pacific. But, she wasn't ready to take that chance yet. Wounds from childhood pains ran too deep, leaving emotional scars. She sighed and turned back to the kitchen.

How could they be prepared for the lunch crowd? Even if Mr. Hastings brought Mrs, Mayer back immediately, getting lunch prepared would be a miraculous feat. Tabby glanced at the stove. No, it was better she stay out of the kitchen unless it was for something easy like washing dishes. Nothing she prepared would be palatable, much less suitable for the high standards of a Harvey restaurant, although she did know what good food tasted like.

"Mr. Foster's absence is going to cause a great deal of distress." Miss O'Connor bustled through the kitchen and into the pantry. She reemerged with a sack of coffee beans which she thrust at one of the kitchen helpers. "We need these ground as soon as possible."

"He didn't choose for his mother to become ill." The

head waitress couldn't be so cold as to not care about an ailing woman.

"You're right, of course." Miss O'Connor waved a hand. "Forgive me for seeming so unfeeling. I need you to help Mrs. Mayer with the kitchen staff." She glanced at the clock. "If the woman ever gets here. Where is Mr. Hastings?"

"What about my trainee?"

"She'll have to make do on her own. She seems to be doing fine, and everyone is going to have to pitch in where they're needed." She stormed from the room, muttering something about the manager most likely imbibing in a drink or two.

Tabby scratched her nose. Now what? She hadn't the faintest idea how to run a kitchen. She glanced at the clock. Less than an hour before the lunch crowd would arrive. Fingers of dread snaked through her veins. Oh, where was Mrs. Mayer?

Five faces turned in her direction. One tall, plump girl stepped forward. "I can cook. Not a lot, but there is the beginnings of stew simmering on the stove. If you can slice bread, I'll take over that."

"Oh, bless you." Slicing bread, Tabby could do. Within seconds, the helpers scattered to do their assigned jobs and make sure lunch was on time. They might not have a varied menu, but the food would be good and wholesome. She peered under the lid of the large pot on the stove. The girl obviously didn't know there was little but meat and liquid in the pan.

The fragrant aroma of chicken broth tickled her nose. Her stomach rumbled. After replacing the lid, she stepped back and thought what other ingredients might go with the shredded chicken. "We need chopped carrots and celery, maybe some potatoes. And we need it all within half an hour." She tapped her finger against her lip. *Think, Tabitha. You've eaten plenty of chicken stew in your day.*

She turned to the girl who suggested she slice bread. "What is your name?"

"Dorothy, ma'am. Don't you worry none about the meal. I'm a good cook. Got me eight brothers back home and they are all as hefty as me." The large girl smiled, her eyes all but disappearing in her round cheeks.

"I'm Tabby, and you are a blessing from heaven. I'm going to go tell Miss O'Connor that today's lunch is chicken stew and bread and ask her to advise our customers when they arrive." Then, she needed to slice the bread, make sure there were clean dishes… With her mind ticking off the hundred things she needed to do in a very short amount of time, Tabby pushed into the dining room and made a beeline for the head waitress. "Miss O'Connor."

The head waitress turned, a frown marring her brow. "Please don't tell me there are more complications to this already tiring day."

"No, ma'am." Tabby grinned. "Everything is running smoothly. I've come to tell you that lunch will only be chicken stew and bread, but at least the customers will be fed."

"I'm sure Mr. Hastings won't mind if we offer the one choice as a special of some kind. Maybe charge a lesser price." She nodded. "It's a wonderful idea, Miss McClelland. You're a valuable asset to the Harvey Restaurants."

Tears pricked Tabby's eyes. No one had ever called

her valuable before. In the early years of her childhood, her mother told her she was precious, but endearments and encouraging words were few and far between in her family.

Now, she excelled at something, a job that would provide a good living and a full life. If only Adam's face didn't pop into her mind every time she contemplated a career with the Harvey restaurants.

~

Adam lay in his bunk in the Pullman car, hands folded behind his head, and stared at the ceiling. Worries about his mother and confusion over Tabby had his brain spinning like a drunken twister. Why couldn't life be smooth, going along a track as dependable as the Santa Fe Railroad? He didn't mind the occasional seasonings of a mild upheaval, but he definitely preferred a calm life.

Six months ago he sat down with his family and made their plans to move to San Francisco. He couldn't go ahead with the dream if his mother wasn't a part of it, not after her excitement over opening a Foster family restaurant and bakery. Ma did love making her pastries and passed on her love of cooking to her only son. Adam grinned. Daphne could cook, but nowhere near as good as he or their mother.

He rolled over to his side. He should be home by tomorrow afternoon. His heart leaped, despite the reason for returning. His family was his life. The one important factor, other than God, that Adam could always count on. If only he could add Tabby to that list.

How was the restaurant doing without him? He hated running out in the middle of the day, but family came first. Always. They would manage without him at the restaurant. He shouldn't worry.

He sighed and flopped onto his back. Sleep would arrive as slow as Christmas to a child. Would it help if he dwelled on the memory of his kiss with Tabby? Maybe. He smiled. And maybe thinking of that moment would make sleep even harder to come by.

13

Tabby untied her apron and tossed it into a basket of dirty laundry beside the pantry door. What a long, frantic day. She planted fists on her hips and surveyed the spotless kitchen. She'd done it. Not cook—Mrs. Mayer had shown up by dinner time—but she'd managed, with help, to get lunch served, and the kitchen kept clean.

"It's a good feeling, ain't it?" Mrs. Mayer laid a heavy arm across Tabby's shoulders. "For a little bitty thing, you got a backbone of steel. Not a person here that could've worked harder or done a better job."

"Thank you. It does give me a great feeling of accomplishment." For as far back as she could remember, Tabby didn't think she'd ever been this proud of a day's work. Customers were more than understanding about the absence of a cook at lunch, and happy to pay a reduced price for a simple meal.

"I'm right sorry I wasn't around at lunchtime," Mrs. Mayer said. "But you managed just fine. Besides, from what I've heard, most railroad houses can't give a person a meal even as fine as that chicken stew." She removed her arm and untied her apron, then tucked it into a bag under the counter. "I'll be here early in the morning to help with breakfast."

Tabby grinned. "I'll be here."

Mrs. Mayer laughed. "I know you will. Good night." She hustled out the back door, leaving Tabby in a sudden silence that hurt her ears.

Without the day's busyness, Adam's absence assaulted her. She would have loved for him to see her accomplishment. He would have given her that wide grin of his and said how proud he was.

She banged out the door. Locusts buzzed, and crickets chirped, adding their songs to the music played by the evening breeze. Tabby closed her eyes and leaned against the warm wood of the restaurant.

Nothing soothed and calmed better than time spent quietly in God's creation. She glanced toward the gazebo, white in the moonlight. Muted conversation drifted from that direction. She squinted trying to see who was enjoying a nighttime tryst.

She couldn't see well enough and turned her attention to the night sky. Did Adam look upon the same stars and moon and think of her, or did he sit beside his mother's sickbed and ache with worry? Tabby prayed he hadn't been welcomed with bad news.

Life held nothing more important for Tabby than Adam's friendship. If he was unable to return to Topeka, she'd have to move along without delay. Kansas held too many memories of the handsome cook, always ready with a smile and a listening ear.

Her heart sank as she thought of that morning. Clearly he'd wanted a word of encouragement from her. Something that told him she cared. She couldn't. She wasn't ready to hand a man her heart. What if she never was?

Did she want to be a head waitress? The day's events proved she had the capability of making decisions under pressure. The head waitress's pleasure had been evident in the pleased glances sent Tabby's way throughout the day.

She rested her elbows on her knees. Folks didn't seem to look kindly on a woman working outside the home. Women were meant to have a husband and children, not a job. Sure, teachers worked, but quit once they married, same as a Harvey Girl. Tabby traced an A in the dirt with her shoe.

Since married women weren't allowed to work in most places, did that mean marriage was a woman's lot in life? She groaned and scuffed away the letters of Adam's name. What was she doing allowing such thoughts? She was the daughter of a womanizer, having nothing of value to bring to a man, much less an upstanding one like Adam with dreams of owning his own restaurant. If she married him, and people found out about her less than respectable childhood, it might reflect badly on Adam. Tabby didn't want to risk his being shunned or disrespected. No, she was better suited to remain alone.

Someone once told her that a woman always married a man just like her daddy. Well, not Tabby. That held absolutely no appeal.

A woman's voice raised in anger drew Tabby's

attention back to the gazebo. She got to her feet and stepped into the shadows, not meaning to eavesdrop, but not wanting to go inside in case someone needed her.

"Stop!"

Someone definitely needed her. Tabby glanced around for a weapon, finding nothing but a fist-sized stone. Better than nothing. She grasped the rock and made her way along the edge of the building.

"I said no, and I meant it!"

Tabby gasped as she realized the voice belonged to the head waitress. Miss O'Connor stood in the embrace of Mr. Hastings, averting her face.

"I won't kiss you until you promise to stop making eyes at every girl that comes through the restaurant."

"Gertie, it's only you that's important to me." He tried again to kiss her. "I promise. The others mean nothing. It's a mature woman I want."

Miss O'Connor's teeth flashed in the light of the moon. Tabby shrank back, not wanting to witness a lover's spat that showed signs of cooling in anger and heating in ardor.

Clapping a hand over her mouth to stifle her gasps, she fled back to the building. Never in a month of Sundays would she have believed Miss O'Connor would put up with a philandering man. She sagged against the wall. Maybe that's all life had to offer. A woman tied herself to one man, while the man found pleasure with any number of women. After all, the men in the Old Testament had multiple wives. Maybe the desire for more than one woman hadn't been bred out of them.

Tears poured down her face. Maybe Adam would be

like her pa and Mr. Hastings, unable to help it any more than Tabby could help being a McClelland.

~

Adam bounded from the buckboard and sprinted up the stairs to his family home, leaving the neighbor to drop his bag on the porch as the man saw fit. "Daphne! Pa!"

"Here, Adam." His little sister, a diminutive blond who barely reached his chin launched herself at him. "Ma is resting. Come have something to eat."

"Okay. You can fill me in on the details." He followed her into the kitchen and swung a chair around backward before straddling it. He focused his gaze on his sister's freckled face. "What's the matter with Ma?"

Daphne poured him a glass of milk. "She started having trouble breathing about a month ago. When she got worse, Pa fetched the doctor. We thought it was a cold at first, now it appears she's got pneumonia." She turned to the stove where she took a pan and dumped its contents onto a plate then set it in front of him. "I cooked you some eggs."

"Thanks." He stared at the food. "Is she going to die?"

"I don't know. She's pretty bad off. Doc says if she lives, we should get her to the coast as soon as we can." Her voice shook. "There may be something around here she's allergic to."

"She'll live." He shoved the plate away without taking a bite and leaped to his feet. Ma dying wasn't an option. "I'll figure out how to get the money we need somehow. Where's Pa?"

"Trying to figure out how many cattle to sell. We've only got the bull and a few cows." She sniffed. "We're down to the bare minimum in livestock. Pa's getting rid of everything he can to raise the money."

"I've got a few hundred dollars set aside. Do you think we can do three more months?" He'd make sure they had the money if he had to work a second job. "What makes the doc think the ocean air will be better for Ma than the air in Missouri?"

"He doesn't know. Only that Ma talks about the ocean all the time." Daphne plopped into a chair and rested her forehead on her arms. "That's what makes me think she's going to die and that she wants to see the ocean before that happens." "Stop talking like that." Adam shoved back his chair and stormed from the room. In the hall, he stopped and struggled to slow his breathing. It wouldn't do to see Ma with fear raging through him.

He took a deep breath, pushed open her door, and stepped inside the dim room. Heavy curtains hung where once sheers allowed light in. A mound of thick quilts covered his mother's body. Adam slid the curtains apart an inch or two to let in some afternoon light, then pulled the room's one chair, a rocker Pa built, to the side of the bed. He took his mother's hand in his. "Ma? I'm here."

"Son." The word wheezed from her. "Open the curtains wide. Let me see you."

He jumped to do her bidding and blinked against the sun's glare. "Are you sure? It's bright."

"Yes. Help me sit up."

Every word she forced from tortured lungs tore at him. "What can I do?"

"Nothing. I'll be fine. I'm just tired."

"It's pneumonia, Ma." Adam fluffed the pillows and

added an extra one so she could recline.

"Pshaw. That doctor doesn't know anything. It's been the same thing off and on my whole life."

Adam sat back in the rocker. "It's bad enough that Daphne's worried sick herself. I haven't spoken to Pa yet."

She coughed hard enough to shake the bed. "You shouldn't be here. You should be working so we can move."

"Why are you in such a hurry? You need to get well first. California isn't going anywhere."

"Son, I'm getting old. I've always wanted to see the ocean. It's as simple as that."

He shook his head. Nothing was ever that simple with Ma. She had something up her flannel sleeve besides a handkerchief. He squeezed her hand. "Tell me the truth, Ma."

"I am." She averted her face.

"Ma."

"Fine." She crossed her arms looking exactly as Daphne had at the age of ten. "I want some adventure before the Lord takes me home."

Adam laughed. "I know someone else who wants adventure. She's one of the girls I work with. You'd like her. You're a lot alike." He glanced out the window. Waves of wheat shined gold in the afternoon sun. He'd miss his childhood home, but his heart leaped at knowing California waited.

"Is she pretty?" Ma wiggled her eyebrows.

"Very." Adam stood. "Now, you behave and rest. I'm going to find Pa." After planting a kiss on her forehead, he left the room and headed out the back door.

Pa led a yearling colt out of the barn. "Son, you made it. Sorry I didn't meet you at the station. Found a buyer for Little Red."

"You aren't selling all the stock, are you, Pa?" Adam hoped not. He'd miss the big red stallion Pa had raised from a baby and Ma's dapple grey mare with the gentle eyes. He glanced around for his dog. "Where's Twister?"

"She's in the barn nursing her latest litter."

Adam clapped his Pa on the shoulder then trotted to the barn. When Adam left home, Pa had brought home a dog of mixed breed that shook her tail so hard at times Adam thought she'd twist in half. Hence her name. They'd been friends since Adam's first visit back. He'd fallen in love with the silky haired mutt. A sharp bark welcomed him to the barn and the black and brown brindled dog bounded to his side. Four yipping pups stumbled after her.

Adam knelt on the packed dirt floor and held out his arms. "My girl!" He laughed and fell back when eighty pounds of dog crashed into him.

"You're such a kid." Daphne stepped from one of the stalls, grinning. "So, big brother. Got a special girl in Kansas?"

14

Saturday night, Tabby lugged buckets of hot water to the room set aside for the women's bathing, while other waitresses prepared to enjoy visits in the parlor with gentlemen or a leisurely time of window shopping. Such a glamorous life she lived.

After she'd dumped the last bucket into the tub, she laid her hands on the small of her back and leaned back, popping the kinks from her spine. While the water cooled, she undressed then removed the pins from her hair. Maybe the other girls did go into town, but a leisurely bath sounded like heaven to Tabby.

She stepped into water almost hot enough to burn, and reached for a bar of rose-scented soap. With a sigh, she lowered herself until only her head remained above the water. It might be a silly indulgence, but she let the bar of soap float in order to send its fragrant tendrils through the water.

Laying her head back against the tub's rim, she allowed thoughts of Adam to drift into her mind. Monday would be a week since he left and no one had heard a word from him. She supposed she could ask Mr. Hastings if he knew anything, but the thought of talking to the weasel made her skin crawl. Maybe there was a way to ask Miss O'Connor that wouldn't show Tabby was aware of the woman's relationship with the manager.

As the water started to cool, she lathered her arms with the soap, then slid her entire body under the water. She'd smell like flowers for nobody. She might as well get used to the idea that rose scented soap would be primarily for her own enjoyment. But she really did miss Adam very much, and the thought scared her. When he wasn't around, loneliness consumed her despite the busy days. Not very encouraging for her vow to remain unmarried.

She sat up and let a few tears of self-pity fall. What a silly girl she was. Either she wanted a relationship with a man or she didn't. Why so many questions? She'd made her choice after all. She and Adam could be nothing but friends.

The door knob jiggled mere seconds before a knock pounded on the door. "Hurry up!" Merrilee's shrill voice disturbed the peace. "Other people need baths. Why is the door locked?"

Tabby sighed, stood, and reached for her towel. After wrapping it around her, she padded to the door and threw the latch. "Sorry."

There were three curtained off areas for the women to bathe and they weren't supposed to lock the door to prevent the others from coming in. But the promise of relaxation and peace won out, at least temporarily, and Tabby had ignored the rule.

Once the door was unlocked, Merrilee shoved her way in. "I'm informing Miss O'Connor of you breaking yet another rule. Eventually her favoritism toward you will wane." She stomped her feet. "I'm going to be late for a dinner engagement because of you."

"You knocked for less than a minute." Tabby drew her curtain then replaced her towel with a robe. With Merrilee gone for the evening, she could curl up in the parlor with a good book and the small box of chocolates she had bought yesterday evening. She smiled at the knowledge that the other girl seemed to have transferred her attentions from Adam to some other unsuspecting fool.

Merrilee grabbed an empty bucket. "They should have someone draw our baths. It takes way too long to do it ourselves."

"How many servants did you have at home?" Tabby cocked her head. Somehow she would find out that Merrilee wasn't the daughter of a once prosperous plantation owner.

"About twenty." Merrilee smiled.

"That isn't very many field workers." Tabby tightened her sash.

"Oh, I meant to say we had twenty house servants."

"You must have been very young during the war." Tabby put a hand on the door. "It's surprising how much you can remember of your life then." With a satisfactory slam, she closed the door.

She really shouldn't let the other girl sour her attitude, but she couldn't help it. Merrilee would have been about two years old when the war ended. No way would she know how things used to be. If not for books, Tabby wouldn't know herself. People shouldn't put on airs.

Back in her room, she dressed in a simple yellow calico dotted with blue, braided her damp hair, then pinned it in a bun. Presentable, she made her way to the parlor, which thankfully, was empty. Grabbing a copy of *Anna Karenina*, she settled into an overstuffed chair and prepared to get engrossed in a new novel.

Adam's face and blue eyes swam across the page until she sighed and laid the book in her lap. What could she do to rid her mind of him? What if he stayed in Missouri on his family's farm or headed west without returning to Topeka? Would she spend the rest of her life seeing him in everything she did?

She stood and moved to the window and stared down at the train platform. The night was quiet. Maybe she should have taken a stroll down Topeka's Main Street or joined a group of fellow waitresses for a night of frivolity. Her shoulders slumped. Or maybe she would have been lonelier than now. Mingling with the masses set a person up for rejection. Something she had had plenty of in her life.

A couple, hand in hand, stood under a gaslight. Tabby leaned her forehead against the cool glass of the window. They looked happy and in love. The gentleman's attention seemed riveted on the woman. How long until he broke her heart?

Tabby wanted to go back in time and warn her mother of the heartache to come. Tell her of Pa's future actions and implore her to marry another. Occasionally, Ma had spoken of another man, a kinder man, who had professed his love once upon a time, but Pa's handsome face had won out in the end.

With a deep breath, Tabby let the drapes fall, shutting out sight of the lovers. Retrieving her book, she headed upstairs where her bed waited. One comforting thing she could rely on.

~

Adam propped a booted foot on the porch railing and stared overhead. Less than a week and Ma was doing fine. He'd catch a train back to Topeka, and Tabby, tomorrow.

"Eager to get back to your girl?" Ma stepped beside him, a thick quilt wrapped around her thin shoulders.

The night breeze had a slight chill to it, but not enough for Adam to go running for a coat. He wrapped the blanket tighter around his mother's shoulders. "She isn't my girl."

"Would you like her to be?" Ma lowered herself into a rocker.

"Yeah, I would." He faced her, leaning against the railing. A bull frog croaked from the pond in back of the house. "But she's had some pain in her life and doesn't have much faith in men."

"Then you have to give her some." Ma set the rocker into motion. "Show her how love can be between a man and a woman. The beautiful thing God created it to be."

"I'm trying, and while she's content to be my friend, even looks forward to our conversations, something holds her back." She had a wall around her heart he wasn't sure he would ever be able to knock down. "You and Pa have such a special marriage. How do you keep the love alive?"

"By putting the other one first." Pa came up the steps, stomping the mud from his feet. "Not hard to do when your bride is as lovely as mine." He placed a kiss on Ma's cheek. "No fever. You're healing."

"Yes, I am, praise God." She squeezed Pa's hand, then once he entered the house, turned back to Adam. "It's the little things, son, that capture a woman's heart. A tender look, a small gift, the brush of a hand, seeing God's love shine through you. These are the things that make her take notice. Try it. She'll fall in love with you in no time. Now help me up so I can go to bed."

"Thanks for the advice, Ma." Adam held out a hand. She grasped it and he pulled her to her feet. "You're a true treasure."

Rising on tiptoe, she kissed his cheek. "That's what mothers are for." She cupped his face. "I love you, son, and want you to find the same happiness I did. Pray about this girl. If she's the one for you, God will make it happen."

Adam intended to do just that. He'd surround Tabby with so much prayer and fond gestures, she'd be weak kneed and mad with love. Maybe mad wasn't the right word. He laughed remembering the way her eyes flashed when something aggravated her. Well, he'd make her fall in love with him if it was the last thing he did.

Quick strides took him to the corral. Pa promised last night they'd be taking Twister and the two horses to California. Once Adam had the money saved, his family would hop a train, boarding the horses in the livestock car, and meet him on the coast.

He leaned against the fence. That gave him four or five months, to his calculations, to convince Tabby to marry him. All of his wooing would have to be at a relatively low cost or he'd set the whole family back in their plans. Thankfully, prayers were free. Once he neared his financial goal, he'd wire Pa to sell the farm. Sure would be nice to have a bride to celebrate the accomplishment with him—or at least a fiancee.

"Nice night." Pa strolled up beside him. "Even nicer now that your Ma is doing better."

Adam stared into the night sky so laden with stars he felt as if he might be able to reach up and pluck one. "Will you miss it here?"

"Nah." Pa rested his elbows on the top corral rail. "I'm ready for a change. This land was your Grandpa's dream, not mine. Not that I don't love it, but there's riches to be had out west, I've heard, and a change will be good for Ma."

"I hope so." Adam turned. He could barely make out his Pa's features in the dark. "It will still be hard work."

"Work is good for a man. Found us a buyer when it's time. Offering a fair price, too. He's also buying Old Man Wilson's farm for the water rights, I reckon."

"I'm saving every penny I can. I figure four or five months."

"Plenty of time to win that gal's heart." Pa chuckled. "I overheard you talking to your ma. She wasn't as willing to marry a farmer as she lets on. For a while, I thought she might take up with the banker's boy. Scared me a bit."

Adam couldn't see his ma with anyone but Pa, any more than he could envision himself with any other woman but Tabby. "Thanks." He clapped Pa on the shoulder. "Between the advice I got from you and Ma, I can't go wrong. Tabby will be a great asset to our restaurant."

"Don't tell her that, even if it is true. During the

courting period, women only want flowery words, not sensible talk. You tell her how much she can help in our new venture and you might scare her off."

"I don't think so, but I'll take your words into account. She wants adventure. What's more adventurous than starting up a business in a new place?" Adam stared back at the pasture.

"Marriage, son. That's the greatest adventure." Pa laughed again and moseyed back toward the house.

Adam figured he was right. Now to convince Tabby.

15

"Why the sudden change of heart toward me a few weeks back?" Tabby waited next to Miss O'Connor while the train pulled into the station with its usual puff of steam and shrill whistle. "I've meant to ask before, but time hasn't permitted." The head waitress seemed almost friendly now, and the numbers on Tabby's badge continued to drop, signifying her satisfying job performance.

The other woman shrugged. "You're more than capable of doing your job with little help from me. Seems maybe the old adage about bees, honey, and vinegar might have some truth to it after all." She smiled. "And a more positive attitude did gain me a box of chocolates, did it not?"

Tabby laughed. "Yes, ma'am, it did." She supposed having two waitresses run off within a few days of each other might have opened the woman's eyes a bit, too.

She tucked a few stray strands of hair back into her bun and prepared to greet the customers who would soon surge through the doors.

"You keep up the good work," Miss O'Connor said. "And you'll have your pick of restaurants in no time." She stepped forward and opened the dining room door as passengers disembarked from the train.

Her pick of placements! Tabby's heart leaped. Her dream could come true sooner than she thought. Restaurants were popping up all along the Santa Fe railroad with the regularity of the seasons. Why, a girl could move every six months and experience something new.

The door swung open, and Tabby's mouth dropped open. Trying her best to hide a grin she knew must cover half of her face, she worked to stop from bouncing on her toes. He was back, bringing an extra ray of sunshine into the room with his smile.

Adam dropped his bag beside the nearest table and headed toward her, completely alerting her to the fact she might not succeed at her plans. Not if she let her emotions get in the way.

"You're back." She couldn't breathe. Her heart raced faster than a tornado crossing the prairie. "I wasn't sure if you would return."

He took her hands in his, his eyes darkening. "Of course I would. You're here. There's no way I could stay away for long. I meant to come back yesterday, but my folks wanted me to stay and attend church with them. Did you miss me?"

Oh, my. He came back for her. Her face flushed. She needed to change the direction of their conversation before it became entirely inappropriate. "How is your mother?"

"Good. Anxious to move..We were pretty worried for a bit, but Ma's stronger than she looks and pulled through just fine." He dropped her hands leaving them feeling as cold as a winter wind. "I'm glad to see you managed without me."

"Barely." So, he'd be moving soon, now that his mother was better. Her eyes stung. She turned so he wouldn't see. She should be happy for him. She forced her voice to remain calm and busied her hands gathering menus. She refused to marry him, so why did she ache at knowing he would leave? "Mrs. Mayer filled in fulltime by the second day. I ran the kitchen in between."

"You?" Adam laughed. "Maybe I'm rubbing off on you."

"Hardly. We kept the lunches simple and offered folks a special price to compensate for the lack of meal choices." Composure in place, she turned. "I'm sure Mrs. Mayer will be very happy to see you."

"Great. I'll go relieve her now." He laid a hand on her shoulder then retrieved his bag and rushed into the kitchen.

Tabby's shoulder burned where he touched her, and she waited until he was out of sight before wiping away a tear. What a sad state she found herself in. She could tell herself until her face turned blue that she didn't want anything more than friendship from him, but it was all a lie. How could she be so scared of such a kind man?

Pa was probably kind at one time or Ma would never have married him, would she? Tabby glanced to where Merrilee stood at attention next to a table. She didn't appear to need Tabby's assistance so she transferred her attention to making sure pewter pitchers were full of cool water and hot coffee waited to be poured.

Now that she no longer carried heavy platters of food all day, the former ever-present fog of exhaustion stayed away for the most part. If only she could uncloud her mind and heart as easily.

Soon, the chatter of customers and the clink of silverware against china plates filled the restaurant. Tabby smiled. What a wonderful place to work. She didn't mind the long hours, or the condescending attitude of some of the customers. Well, not much anyway. She only needed to worry about God's opinion of her choice of job. Someday folk's eyes would be open and willing to accept women entering the workforce. Even people like Pastor Harper.

Yesterday, she'd gotten ready for church. Even went so far as to walk to the clapboard building. But, she didn't enter. She couldn't. Not as long as Pastor Harper still preached there.

She wrapped her hands around the handles of the drink cart and pushed it to the first table. Her stomach dropped. Pastor Harper sat, newspaper in front of him, his gaze following the girls as they glided past his table, as if they were on the menu. Maybe Tabby could pour his coffee and move on without receiving a lecture.

After filling his mug, she turned to leave and released the breath she'd been holding.

"Wait a minute."

She cringed. Why her? The room was full of others for him to torment. Swallowing past the mountain in her throat, she turned.

"Do you have no shame?"

"Pardon me?"

"A woman should serve no man but her husband, yet you pour me coffee in a very familiar way, even allowing your skirt to brush my leg." His mouth turned down at the corners.

"It's familiar because I've poured hundreds of cups of coffee, sir, and wear a full skirt." Tabby straightened her shoulders. She'd put this man in his place once and for all. "It's my job."

"Hell fire waits for wanton women." He smirked. "But I could be enticed to say a prayer on your behalf."

"How dare you." Tabby's fingers curled around the handle of the water pitcher.

"Isn't that why the women are here? To find a man?" He crossed his arms. "I choose you."

"That will never happen."

"Women working outside the home is not a pleasing aspect. You should be satisfying your husband, raising children, and running a home."

"I need to please no one but God." She prayed for God to restrain her from dumping the water on his head.

"You are not fit to speak his name." Harper stood, bumping the table. His coffee sloshed onto the white tablecloth leaving brown droplets scattered like polka dots.

Tabby lost all restraint and upended the pitcher on his head.

~

Adam froze in the kitchen doorway. Tabby really did dump water on the pastor's head. He didn't imagine it. He stifled a grin as she stomped her foot and stormed outside. Obviously the man had said something personally derogatory.

After the last two sermons Adam forced himself to sit through, he'd hoped someone would put the man in his place; he just didn't expect it to be a slip of a girl. He placed a plate of sourdough biscuits on the counter, then followed her outside.

He found her around the corner, arms wrapped around her waist, hunched over, and crying. "Tabby?" Without thinking, he pulled her close and nestled her head in the crook of his shoulder. "What happened?"

"He called me wanton, then proceeded to tell me he chose me out of the other girls." She lifted a tear-streaked face. "That is not a man of God!"

"No, Tabby, it isn't." He nestled her head back to where it fit as naturally as breathing.

"Is it so wrong for a woman to work?"

"No, and times are changing. Fred Harvey saw a need that benefited everyone. If people only knew how well chaperoned the ladies are, how morally upstanding, they'd change their outlook. Be patient. A new way of thinking is coming." Tabby felt as if she belonged in his arms. Her curves fit his planes. He closed his eyes and laid his cheek on top of her head. The scent of roses wafted from her hair.

"Aren't there any honorable men?" She sniffed, then pulled back, and palmed the tears from her eyes.

What about him? Did she look at him so much as a friend that she couldn't see him as a man? "Me. My Pa. I could give you a list."

She sighed. "A short list."

"But a list nevertheless." He gripped her shoulders and forced her to look at him. "All men are not bad, Tabby. Most of them are good. You, unfortunately, have seen more than your share of the bad." How would she react if he told her of his failure to keep Marilyn alive? Would she add him to the list of unworthy men?

She wrenched herself out of his grip. "All the ones I know are, present company excluded. Even now, you lay hands on me to get my attention."

"Never in anger, Tabby. Never." He shook his head and blinked against the stinging sensation. "Or with inappropriateness. I care far too much for you."

"So you say at this moment." She shook her head. "I'm sorry. I let Harper's words affect me more than I should have. My mother tried to teach me that the opinion of other people shouldn't matter. But it does, sometimes." With a visible struggle to contain herself, she gave a firm nod, then spun to go back to the restaurant.

Her walking away cast a cloud over the day. He needed to head back to the kitchen, but instead leaned against the rough wood of the train depot and prayed for Tabby's pain and for her to gain a renewed faith in men. Him in particular. How could he gain her trust and win her love if she shied away from him? He wished there was a way for her to see how his parents interacted with each other.

The train whistle blew. The passengers would be reboarding. Adam pushed away from the wall. Stepping to the platform, he noticed a very wet Pastor Harper boarding. Good riddance. Maybe by Sunday, they'd have a new pastor. One who wasn't as narrow minded.

Adam kicked a rock onto the train track. He wanted to get involved in church. For the first time since reaching adulthood he wasn't helping mentor younger believers. Maybe, if they did get a new pastor, he could convince Tabby to help him in his ministry. That would be a way to spend approved time together, hopefully without a chaperone.

As he passed through the restaurant on his way to the kitchen, he tossed Tabby what he thought was a reassuring smile. He hoped it didn't look as sad as he felt. He could only hope his efforts to win her would not be in vain. A sharp pain stabbed his heart, and he gasped.

He needed to give her over to God. But could he?

On his way to the kitchen, Adam grabbed his apron from a hook beside the kitchen door, and then marched to the counter where one of his helpers chopped potatoes. Another stirred a pot of brown gravy. He almost felt unneeded now that the restaurant was fully staffed. Other than conferring with Hastings and Miss O'Conner about the menu, he mostly delegated tasks.

Once he owned his own restaurant, all that would change. He tied his apron around his waist and donned his chef hat. He could easily see Tabby working beside him at Foster's Eatery. With her pretty face greeting customers, they'd have more work than they could handle. Of course, Daphne's youthful exuberance wouldn't hurt either.

He directed one of the busboys to take fresh coffee out to the drink girls. The boy loaded several pitchers of boiling water onto the rolling cart, then barreled through the swinging doors, knocking a stack of baskets over on his way out. A few minutes later, he returned for more hot water.

"Slow down, son." Adam waved a wooden spoon in his direction. "And pick up those baskets."

"Right away, sir." The boy nodded hard enough for a curl of his dark hair to fall forward over his eyes. "As soon as I take in the last of this water." He dashed away, sending the cart careening ahead of him.

A loud clatter alerted the rest of the staff to catastrophe.

Someone screamed.

16

Scalding water splashed against Tabby's legs, soaking her stockings and the hem of her uniform. She sagged against the counter and bit her lip.

The poor busboy crawled around her feet, sopping up the spilled water. Despite her pain, a chuckle escaped Tabby when he went to lift her skirts to dab at her legs. "That's quite all right, thank you, I can manage from here."

Miss O'Connor took her by the arm and led her into the kitchen. "No sense in entertaining the customers." She helped Tabby into a chair beside the work island. "Remove your stockings immediately, Miss McClelland. Mr. Foster, a pail of cool water and a clean towel, please."

Tabby removed her shoes and stockings then hid her face in her hands. Mortification burned hotter than the water when Miss O'Connor slid up her skirts and applied cold compresses to her legs. Such a ninny to carry on so, screaming and practically collapsing in full view of the restaurant. Now, Adam knelt beside the head waitress to make her embarrassment complete.

"I'm fine," she mumbled through her fingers. "Really, I am."

"Your skin is red and inflamed. Straight to bed. I'll send up some ointment at the first opportunity." Miss O'Connor straightened. "Mr. Foster, please assist Miss McClelland."

Tabby jerked upright. "But, Miss O'Connor, it wouldn't be proper." Heaven have mercy. He'd seen way too much of what he shouldn't already.

"I'm not asking the man to enter your room, only to make sure you make it that far." She waved her hand. "Go on, now."

Adam grasped her arm and helped her stand. The coolness of the kitchen's tile floor eased some of the pain in her feet. If only she could lay her flushed cheeks against the polished floor or possibly sink out of sight altogether.

"Should I carry you?" The concern on Adam's handsome face brought tears to her eyes.

"No, I can manage, thank you. Really, there's no need for you to accompany me. I'll go to my room, change, and be back at work in a moment."

"Oh, no, you will not." Miss O'Connor crossed her arms. "We can manage a day without you. After all, we managed without Mr. Foster for several days."

"But not because of his clumsiness." Tabby pulled free of Adam's grasp. "I am perfectly fine. I will change, spread ointment on the burned areas, and return to work." Head held high, shoes and socks gripped tightly in her hand, Tabby marched from the kitchen and up the stairs, ignoring the pain in her shins. She would not show weakness after acting so foolishly brave.

From the heavier steps behind her, she knew without looking that Adam trailed after. "This isn't necessary." She stopped and placed her hand on the door frame.

"It is." He strolled toward her. "I care for you. It hurts me when you are injured."

She turned her head, unwilling to see the pain in his eyes. "We can't do this, Adam."

"Why? What?" With his index finger, he turned her face toward his.

"This." She waved an arm. "We want different things from life. You can't keep jumping to my aid."

"I can. I will." A muscle ticked in his jaw.

"You are jeopardizing our friendship." Couldn't he see that? By requesting something more, he threatened what they had.

"I'm no longer content to just be friends."

"Then you've made the decision to dissolve our relationship." Tabby stepped into her room and closed the door. After a few moments, his footsteps receded. She threw herself across her bed and sobbed.

~

Adam stomped down the stairs, fighting the urge to punch the wall. Infuriating woman! All he wanted to do was help her. He'd caught a glimpse of her legs before he averted his gaze. The red skin had looked tender. Why couldn't she let him help her?

When she'd screamed, he'd thought of nothing but to get to her side. Miss O'Connor had beat him, but Adam had hovered like a nervous mother. Or a man in love.

Back in the kitchen, he ignored the curious glances of his staff and banged pans while preparing lunch. Let them stare. He owed no one an explanation.

Once he had stew bubbling and a roast in the oven, he barged out the back door and stared in the direction of the woods. His conversation upstairs with Tabby effectively put a halt to their evening conversations, of that he had no doubt. What an idiot he was. Why couldn't he have moved slower? Courted her more?

Show her what a good man is like, Ma said. How could he when she didn't want him around? There had been moments before his trip home when he'd actually thought they were making progress in their relationship. How mistaken he was.

If only he had the money to head to California, but he was a few months short. If Pa got a good price for the farm, and was able to rent the house back from the new owner, maybe Adam could leave sooner than planned. He'd send a telegram home tomorrow.

He shouldn't waste any more time on a woman who didn't want him. Tabitha McClelland was ripping his heart apart, piece by piece. Soon, a big wind would blow him away.

~

Tabby blew her nose and splashed water from the porcelain basin on her dresser on her face. She needed to avoid Adam. The ever present pain in his eyes would be her undoing.

A knock sounded on the door. She dried her face and padded barefoot to the door. "Who is it?"

"Maggie from the kitchen."

Tabby opened the door to a child of maybe fourteen. The girl thrust a metal canister and bandages at Tabby.

"Here. The wagon boss sent it." She whirled and dashed away.

Tabby's legs stung, but the healing balm would bring welcome relief. She sat in a chair and hefted her skirts above the knee. "It doesn't look that bad." She popped the lid to the small can and dug her fingers into a greasy substance that smelled like cut grass.

Hissing against the pain, she spread a thick film on her legs, then wrapped then in white cotton before donning fresh stockings. She wouldn't scar, and most likely by tomorrow, her legs would feel as if she'd never gotten burned.

Next time, she'd stay away from the door until making sure no one was going to barrel through. If only keeping her eyes open and paying attention would resolve her conflict with Adam as easily. She would miss his company.

Tears started fresh. What a cruel joke life played. Send her a man that might prove all men weren't scoundrels, but put such a fear in Tabby's heart, she couldn't risk finding out. Her gaze fell on the Bible beside her bed.

Tonight, she'd search God's Word for answers.

17

Tabby watched as Adam chopped ice. She wrapped her shawl tighter around her against the brisk fall wind. They'd all prayed for a continuation of an Indian summer, but obviously God had other plans. She turned away when Adam glanced her way.

With her contract expiring in a little over a month, she'd taken to avoiding him, even forgoing their nightly chats on the back stoop. There was no sense in encouraging him. After all, he'd be leaving soon, and so would she.

Weeks ago he'd approached her about helping minister to the church's youth. It had taken some convincing on his part that the new pastor was nothing like the last. While she loved the opportunity to minister, it brought her in close proximity to him. She didn't think her heart could take much more.

"We need more ice." Annie, one of the older girls

shivered next to her. "And it's freezing."

"We'll have to move the ice cream social into the fellowship hall." Tabby tucked a stray strand of the girl's auburn hair behind her ear. At least there was little chance of the ice melting too quickly. "Why don't you get a couple of the stronger boys to carry things inside?"

She grinned. "Yes, ma'am. And I know just the two to do it." She dashed away.

Tabby chuckled. Most likely the girl ran off to Bo, a handsome young man she appeared to have her eye on for some time. Her laughter faded. Oh, to be that young. On days like today, when her thoughts were heavy, Tabby felt much older than her nineteen years.

Maybe she should have sent Annie to fetch the ice, and inform the boys herself. Now, she'd have to speak to Adam. His demeanor toward her lately had been anything but warm, not that she blamed him. Poor man was obviously confused by her cooling manner toward him.

Ducking her head against the wind, she set off with strong strides, stopping just out of reach of flying ice shards. Without speaking, she knelt and started tossing them into a nearby bucket.

"It's unusually cold today." Adam straightened, the ax hanging by his side.

"Yes, it is." So, their conversations had fallen to trivial matters like the weather. It was for the best, she figured. "We're moving the social inside. I doubt the church members will mind."

"Probably not." He sighed. "Heard Mr. Harvey arrives tomorrow with a new manager."

Tabby glanced up, forgetting her resolve not to make

eye contact. "A new manager, why?"

"It's just a rumor, but I've heard there have been too many complaints from the girls about Mr. Hastings' behavior." His gaze searched her face, looking for something she wasn't ready to give. "The man's had it coming, in my opinion."

A shadow crossed his features. "Go get out of the wind. I'll bring the ice."

Miss O'Connor had mentioned in passing the other day that one of the other restaurants needed a girl to fill in for a week. Tabby decided she would volunteer. She and Adam needed some time apart for them both to sort out their feelings. With Tabby gone, maybe Adam would realize how futile his aspirations were toward her and find another girl to claim his attention.

So, why did the thought leave her heart crying? Tabitha McClelland was a fool, and she knew it, but she'd dug herself into a hole so big, so deep, she had no idea how to get out.

She stood and dusted off her knees. The church, and the town, seemed proof that loving marriages existed, at least outwardly. Why wasn't she willing to take the chance? Because the McClelland women were unlucky, that's why. Even Grandma had married a scoundrel who spent his day at the saloon, spending every coin he earned on gambling and whiskey. Tabby hitched her skirt and practically sprinted for the church.

Instead of going inside, she dashed around the corner and out of sight. Free from prying eyes, she let her tears fall. God, why couldn't she get over the pain of her childhood? Her mother's mistakes didn't need to be Tabby's as well. Surely, love was free for everyone. She shook her head.

Not free. Love came at a great cost. A cost of submission and risk. She raised her face toward heaven. Why couldn't she pay that cost? Maybe it wasn't that she couldn't, but that she wasn't willing.

Adam called out a greeting to someone. Tabby pressed closer to the church siding. If he caught her crying, he would question her reasons and offer her aid. She banged the back of her head on the wall and struggled to gain control of her emotions.

"Are you in need of assistance?" Mr. Hastings approached, a leer on his thin face. "I can help you, if it's company you need."

Tabby shook her head. "No, thank you. I'm only taking a moment of peace for myself."

"I'll join you." He sidled close until their arms touched. "I'm sure you're aware that I will be leaving soon." He trailed a finger down her cheek. "It would please me to have such a fine looking woman on my arm." The stench of alcohol wafted on his breath.

She pulled away, fighting back nausea. "Please, sir, we're on church ground."

"I found it rather funny when you dumped the water on Pastor Harper, but still thought you needed reprimanding and I thought to add two numbers to your ranking." He straightened. "But decided it was most likely an accident, and decided to forgive you."

"It was no accident." Her hands balled into fists in her pockets. "I'm asking you to leave me alone or regret the consequences."

"Oh, I do like them feisty." He pressed against her. "I bet you taste as sweet as you look." He gripped her face in his hands. "I leave tomorrow. Come with me."

Tabby aimed a kick at his shin and missed. He

pressed harder against her. Bile rose in her throat as he attempted to prove her earlier thoughts untrue about men being able to redeem themselves.

A scream burst from her throat. Mr. Hastings clapped a hand over her mouth. She bit the fleshy part of his palm. He reared back with a roar and laid a strong punch to her jaw.

She crumpled to the ground.

~

When Adam heard Tabby scream, he felt as though someone ripped his heart out. When he saw her on the ground, he knew his heart lay in pieces. He yelled and charged Hastings, tackling the man to the ground, oblivious to the container of cream he still held in his hand. Knowing the woman he loved was in danger, it hadn't occurred to him to dump the cream into the second container for ice cream. Instead, he kept it clutched like a life line and flew outside.

Now, both men rolled on the ground streaked with sticky liquid.

Adam laid a strong uppercut to Hastings's nose. Blood gushed, and mingled with the cream.

"Stop it!" Tabby grabbed at his shirt. "This is a house of God."

Soon, men from church swarmed around them and pulled them apart. Chest heaving, Adam took another step toward Hastings. How dare he strike a woman.

"Adam, please."

He turned to see Tabby, tears running, and an already darkening bruise on her cheek. Without thinking, he pulled her into his arms, unmindful of the blood and cream. He ran his hands down her arms. "Please tell me you aren't injured."

"I'm not." She stepped back and raised a hand to his face, then apparently second guessed touching him. She let her hand drop. "Oh, Adam. Look at you. Look at me. Brawling at church." She waved an arm toward the crowd. "With all the church looking on."

"What would you have me do? He struck you." His shoulders slumped. "I think God would understand in this instance."

Two men helped Hastings to his feet. Adam glared and took a step toward them. One man held up his hand, and Adam stopped. "He isn't worth any more of my time." He grabbed Tabby's arm and marched away, dragging her with him.

"I'm going to clean up. I suggest you do the same, before we finish this ice cream social." He glanced around at the group of young people following them. "Go ahead and finish the ice cream, folks. We'll be back in a few minutes."

He ushered Tabby ahead of him to the restaurant, restraining himself from throttling the silly girl. Couldn't she see how much he cared? That he cared enough to strike another man in her defense?

"Why are you angry with me?" She yanked free. "I did nothing wrong."

"No, you didn't." He turned away. "Everything is as wonderful as it can possibly be. Go change your clothes. I'll meet you back here on the porch in fifteen minutes."

He barged through the door hard enough to bang it against the wall. Not since he was a child had he shown such a degree of temper as today. What he wanted to do was shake some sense into one very stubborn woman. Instead, he'd gain control, change his clothes, and pretend that they were merely friends.

The water in his room's washbasin felt as frigid as his quickly freezing heart. He dropped his clothes in a pile on the floor and splashed his face. Maybe the water's temperature would shock some sense into him.

Why delude himself? He plopped onto his bed. He loved Tabitha McClelland so much he lost all reason. He leaned forward, letting his hands dangle between his knees. But, she didn't return his love. He needed to let her go.

After cleaning himself up and donning a fresh shirt, Adam headed downstairs to wait for Tabby. It would be hard to treat her as a friend when his heart saw her as so much more, but if that was all she had to offer then he would take it. The time for them to go their separate ways would come all too soon.

"There really wasn't a need to wait for me." She stepped out of the parlor.

"It seems you waited for me." He turned and forced a smile.

She shrugged. "I knew you'd wait for quite a while if I weren't here." She took one of his hands in hers, sending his blood racing. "You should have someone tend to your knuckles."

"I hadn't noticed until now." He pulled his scraped hand away and offered his arm instead. Maybe the warmth of her touch wouldn't sear so much through the fabric of his shirt.

They walked back to the church without speaking. Tabby slipped her arm from his and moved to the group of young women while Adam walked with dogged steps to the boys in his charge. Maybe he should let them know that fighting was never the answer.

"You all right, Mr. Foster?" Bo, the brightest and rowdiest of the group, approached him. "You threw a punch for your girl. Why isn't she at your side?"

"I only helped a lady in distress. She isn't my girl."

"Your face says otherwise." He handed Adam a bowl of ice cream.

"God says even more, son." Adam accepted the treat, wishing with all in him that he could share it with Tabby. Of course, he loved the group of boys, but didn't come close to filling a hole made by her.

"Mr. Foster, a word, please?" Pastor Lehman, the kind and godly man chosen to replace Harper, stepped between the boys.

"Of course." Adam nodded to the group and followed the man, fully prepared for a scolding. When they stepped outside, into the thankfully declining wind, Adam faced the pastor. "I'm really sorry for causing a disruption."

"I sincerely doubt you were the cause. You merely came to a lady's aid." The pastor laughed. "I've wanted to punch the man myself a few times."

"You aren't removing me from the ministry?"

"Definitely not. Sit, please." He motioned at the steps. "You seem like a man deeply troubled. I'm wondering whether I can help."

"It's not important." Adam took a seat and placed the bowl next to him.

"I think it is. You look like a man who's lost his best friend."

"I have." Should he tell the pastor everything concerning him? In the grand scheme of things, did the affairs of his heart really matter?

"There's this woman…"

"Ah." Pastor Lehman nodded. "I thought so."

"I love her. She doesn't return the feeling." Adam stared over the lawn. "She has an intense distrust of men. I've tried to show her I'm different, and sometimes I've actually thought I succeeded. But, I haven't."

"The young lady you helped today?"

Adam nodded.

"Unfortunate that Mr. Hastings helped confirm her suspicions. You need to take the matter before God. Put this young woman in His more than capable hands."

"But I'm leaving soon. My family and I are headed to San Francisco."

"You need to tell her of your feelings before you go. Give her something to ponder while you're away. If she loves you, she'll follow, in due time." Pastor Lehman stood. "I will pray for you on a daily basis." He laid a hand on Adam's shoulder. "God promises us the desires of our hearts according to His will."

"Yes, but what if His will doesn't bring me Tabby?"

18

Miss O'Connor poked her head into Tabby's room as she put the finishing touches on her appearance. "Quickly, girls. Mr. Harvey arrives in fifteen minutes." She frowned. "There is a smudge on your shoe, Miss Ramsey, fix it at once." Her heels tapped a hasty retreat as she stopped at each dormitory doorway, calling out for the girls to comb their hair or straighten bed coverings.

"Gracious!" Merrilee swiped at her shoe with a handkerchief. "As if anyone would notice a smudge, the nasty witch."

"She only wants us to be our best." Tabby poked the last hairpin in her hair and took one last glance in the mirror. This was as good as she could get. She ran her hands down her dress, smoothing imaginary wrinkles, and headed for the door. "Best hurry."

Merrilee raced after her. "Don't worry about me."

She passed Tabby and rushed down the stairs.

Again, Tabby doubted the girl came from aristocratic stock. No girl trained in ladylike manners would run down the stairs. She shrugged. She wasn't sure why it bothered her that her roommate appeared to lie about her roots. After all, it was none of Tabby's business. Maybe she was searching for one truthful person in a dishonest world.

Once she reached the restaurant, she moved to Miss O'Connor's side. There was no time like the present to apologize. "I'm terribly sorry about Mr. Hastings' termination."

"Whatever are you talking about?" Miss O'Connor cut her a glance.

"Well, I know that you, and he, uh…"

"You silly girl." Miss O'Connor laughed. "We had nothing serious between us. He was a man to fill an empty spot in my life. I was well aware of his indiscretions. It was I who forwarded the complaints to Mr. Harvey."

"I thought you were in love. I saw the two of you hugging in the gazebo."

Miss O'Connor patted her shoulder. "You really are naïve. Do you get such ideas from that Bible of yours?"

Tabby frowned. "The Bible is a wonderful map for a person's life. I don't believe it silly in the slightest." How could the woman brush aside God's word so easily? Sure, not all people were aware of God's glory, but to call the Bible silly ripped at Tabby's heart.

"Well, my life has shown me differently." The train whistle blew, pulling the head waitress's attention to the front door. "Stand sharp, now. He's coming."

Her life hadn't been that grand either, but it was the

pain and hardship that led her to God, not pulled her away.

"There he is." Miss O'Connor's hand fluttered at her throat. "That must be the new manager with him. He's a fine looking man." She patted her hair.

Hearing the excitement in the other woman's voice, for the first time Tabby studied her as an approachable person. Her features were a bit sharp, and her spectacles tended to slide down her nose, but the brown hair sported no gray streaks and the hazel eyes shone with intelligence. She could see why a man might seek out Miss O'Connor's company.

Tabby switched her attention from the head waitress to the arriving train passengers. One man, slight of build, with a receding hairline, a goatee, and a studious look in his eye, entered the restaurant with a clean shaven man of the same thin stature. "Which one is Mr. Harvey?"

"The bearded man. Smile, he's coming this way."

Tabby turned, folded her hands, and smiled as the two men approached and stopped in front of them.

Mr. Harvey ran his gaze from her shoes to the top of her head, then apparently finding things to his satisfaction, turned to Miss O'Connor. "This is Mr. Edwin Richardson. He will be the new manager, and a great asset to this establishment. I trust Mr. Hastings is no longer with us?"

"Gone on yesterday's train, Mr. Harvey." Miss O'Connor nodded. "We wasted no time after receiving your telegram."

"Very good." A faint Scottish brogue colored his speech. "Upon first impression, I find no fault here, with the restaurant or the girls. I can't wait to taste the food."

"Let me show you to a table, Mr. Harvey. We have one available by the window." Should Tabby bow, curtsy? She felt as if the man were royalty of some kind with the anxious, yet excited, looks everyone threw his way.

"What is your name?"

"Tabitha McClelland, sir."

"Ah, yes." He nodded toward Miss O'Connor. "I've heard many good things about you."

He had? She flicked a glance at Miss O'Connor. She'd spoken about Tabby? The thought filled her with warmth. "I hope my service today lives up to your expectations."

"I'm sure it will. Sit, Richardson. Enjoy a fine meal before I introduce you to who I've heard is the best chef around. I interviewed him in Chicago and was impressed with the man's credentials."

Tabby handed the men menus and took their drink orders. By the time the drink girl poured, Mr. Harvey had ordered two sirloin steak dinners. "A good choice, sir. Mr. Foster makes a fine steak." She nodded and walked briskly to the kitchen. Mr. Harvey would be very pleased with the quality of Adam's cooking.

She paused at the kitchen entrance. Who was she to rejoice with Adam regarding Mr. Harvey's visit? She'd lost that chance days ago when she set him free. There was no one with whom she could share the day's events. No close friends or family.

Shoulder's sagging, she stepped into the kitchen. "Two sirloins with all the fixings."

She hoped Mr. Harvey didn't just sample the food, but took the time to see the kitchen staff in action. She always marveled at the way they each seemed to know what to do, dodging each other like the workings of a clock. They resembled the waitresses only in a much smaller space.

Adam hefted a large pot, his arm muscles bulging as he moved it to the work island. He tossed her a questioning look from under his starched chef hat.

How embarrassing to be caught staring! Much less admiring the physique of a man she couldn't have.

~

Adam delegated many duties, but only he seared steaks to perfection. At least that's what he liked to tell himself, and with the customer being Mr. Harvey, the steaks needed to be perfect. He poked one with his finger to test for tenderness, noted the medium doneness, and grinned.

"Let me serve Mr. Harvey." Merrilee stood by his elbow. "Tabby has enough work and sent me to cover for her."

"Not unless she tells me herself." Adam didn't trust the girl for one second.

"But she did say so." She gripped his arm and pressed against him.

"Miss Ramsey, the help is watching, and I'm busy. Please detach yourself from my arm and stop this embarrassing behavior." He glanced up to see the stony countenance of Tabby.

"Merrilee, your table is requesting your assistance."

The girl sighed with all the drama of a traveling sideshow and barged through the doors to the dining room.

"She said you sent her to wait on Mr. Harvey." Adam grabbed a butcher knife and whacked a head of lettuce.

"I did no such thing." Tabby stomped her foot. "My guess is she's already got her cap set for the new manager."

"I didn't think you'd sent her." *Whack*. The light scent of roses drifted to him, despite the aroma of lunch cooking. Why wouldn't she go away? Instead of sunshine, her presence brought clouds, and he needed to concentrate.

A clatter sounded outside the door. Tabby whirled and dashed away.

Adam set his knife back in its block and followed, worried someone else might be injured.

Merrilee stood with a red face and arms flailing as a busboy knelt on the floor picking up the shattered pieces of a plate. "You imbecile! Look what you've done to my apron." Streaks of gravy marred the stark white.

Tabby moved to help him.

"I'm sorry, miss, but you crashed through the door so fast and…" The young man folded the broken porcelain in his apron.

"Don't make excuses to me. There should be windows in that stupid door, why this isn't…" Merrilee said a few choice words that raised Adam's eyebrows. He motioned for the busboy to head back to the kitchen.

"Miss." Mr. Harvey patted his lips with a napkin and stood. "Please leave this establishment immediately. We do not condone that type of behavior or language under any circumstances."

Tabby handed the busboy the few pieces in her hand and stepped back, eyes wide, and met Adam's gaze. He turned away. Once, they would have spent time discussing the morning's events. No longer. Now, they were no more than fellow employees. They might as well act as such.

Merrilee clasped her hands in front of her. "Please, Mr. Harvey. It was this boy's fault. He's clumsy, and…"

"You made a scene in front of customers." Mr. Harvey shook his head. "It is unacceptable." He motioned to the new manager. "Mr. Richardson, we will conclude with our tour since lunch has been rudely interrupted." He turned to Miss O'Connor. "I do not want to see this young lady again." He turned and marched through the kitchen door.

Merrilee put her hands over her face and sobbed.

Miss O'Conner took her by the arm and pulled her out of view of the dining room, leaving everyone in a state of quiet shock. Adam glanced out of the corner of his eye at Tabby, who stared after Miss O'Connor.

With a heavy heart he headed back to the kitchen to take out his frustration on innocent vegetables. He really needed to leave Kansas. He couldn't bear to see Tabby's face every day.

"How unfortunate." Tabby set an empty tray in the sink after the lunch crowd left.

Adam closed his eyes. She tried so hard to keep up the façade of their friendship. How could she after knowing how he felt about her? Did she have no concern for his feelings?

She leaned against the counter. "She wanted so badly to impress Mr. Harvey and the new manager. Too much, I suppose." She took a deep breath and exhaled loudly. "Well, I can see you're busy." She paused. "I came to let you know that Mr. Harvey has requested my presence at a restaurant in New Mexico. I leave tomorrow."

Leaving? He wanted to ask whether it was a permanent transfer, but couldn't let her know how much her leaving affected him. Moments before he'd convinced himself they'd be better off apart. Now that the opportunity presented itself, all he could think about was missing her with every fiber of his being. He swallowed past the mountain in his throat.

"You must have impressed him." He picked up the menu for dinner. Looking at her would be his downfall.

"Miss O'Connor said I did." He felt her turn. Her voice lowered. "I wanted to let you know, since I'll be leaving on the morning train. I'll be gone for a week. They've also hinted at a promotion. Her lips curled. "That could mean a transfer to a new and exciting place."So, she would return. Foolish man that he proved to be, his heart leaped at the news. No matter what he told himself, he wasn't ready to say goodbye for good. A hinted at promotion wasn't the same as her receiving one. Adam hadn't lost hope yet.

19

With her chin resting in the palm of her hand, and her elbow on the train's window ledge, Tabby watched the restaurant recede from view. Adam rarely spoke to her anymore, even after she told him she would be gone for a week. Most likely it was for the best. They didn't want the same things out of life, and she shouldn't hold him back.

He wanted a family and a home with his parents and sister close by. Tabby didn't know how that felt. From the time she was a child, she had wanted to leave. She hadn't had a destination in mind, just wanted to get away from a melancholy mother and a heavy-handed father. Now, Adam jeopardized everything she thought she wanted out of life.

The possibility of a promotion filled her. She could be sent to the end of the railroad line to a brand new Harvey House. She'd be head waitress and run things her way. What would it be like to be in a place where she belonged? Where she played a major part of what it would require to run a good restaurant?

She didn't need to decide now, but soon. At the latest by the end of her present contract. Would Adam be pleased for her if she received news of advancement?

She craned her neck for one last glimpse of the restaurant, hoping she might catch sight of him. That he might have reconsidered and come to say goodbye. Tears stung her eyes, and she swiped them away with the back of her hand. Her stubbornness and confusion had robbed her of the best friend she'd ever had.

Maybe the week away would help straighten out her feelings. Either that or she'd feel too much time had passed and there would be no way she could apologize.

The clackety-clack of the train lulled her into a doze with sleep induced dreams where she wore frilly gowns and walked through fields of flowers toward Adam. The sun shined, birds sang, and flowers in colors brighter than nature intended surrounded her. Very much like a fairy tale she read once as a child. Except Tabby was no princess to Prince Adam.

She opened her eyes and stroked the plush burgundy arm of the seat. Although the train ride was only her second time in first class, she failed to be excited. No, the fancy surroundings only carried her farther from where she wanted to be.

Strange how it took her leaving to show that Adam held her heart. Sad, that she discovered her feelings for him too late. Depressing that she would have to choose between a career and the love of a man.

~

Dear, God, please open Tabby's heart. Adam

reclined against the outside wall of the restaurant and stared at the stars. With her absence, he'd lost his zeal for his job. His heart ached with missing her.

Like a coward, he'd stayed around the corner and watched as she boarded the train and it pulled away. He should have gone after her, swept her in his arms, and kissed her. He should have made her promise to come back.

Almost a week had passed and he'd heard nothing about whether she would return. Sometimes, girls left to fill in and sent for their things when a permanent position became available. What would he do if that happened with Tabby?

He'd pulled away, and hadn't told her of his feelings, only hinted at them. He needed to tell her that he loved her and then let God handle her response. *Please, let her answer be favorable.*

"Still missing your gal?" The new manager, Richardson, came around the corner. "Not that it's affecting your cooking, but even a stranger such as myself can see your heart is no longer with us."

"No, sir, I reckon it isn't." Adam straightened. "I believe I'll be pulling out soon. Possibly next week."

Richardson nodded. "Not sure we can find a chef in that time, but we'll try."

"Then I'll wait until one arrives, but not a day later."

"Where you headed?"

"San Francisco. My family and I are going to open a restaurant. Pa sold the family farm, and all they're waiting on is me." Adam straightened. "I've enjoyed my time here. The Harvey Company is a fine establishment, but it's time for me to move on." Especially if Tabby returned. Who was he kidding? He couldn't stay even if she remained away. The place held too many memories.

No, he'd follow through with his dream, even if he did so without her by his side. "Think I'll turn in now." He gave a nod to the manager then pushed through the kitchen door.

Most of the time he enjoyed his private accommodations and particularly on that night. Not having to explain his mood to a roommate was priceless. He wanted to wallow in his self-pity alone and away from prying questions or solicitous words of advice.

Tomorrow, he'd send his family a telegram and tell them of his plans to meet in Kansas before heading west. He liked that idea much better than meeting in California. He didn't relish taking the trip alone if Tabby rejected him. He gave himself a mental shake. Why borrow trouble early? The moment his family arrived, Adam planned to jump on the train and proceed with his life. Hopefully, not alone.

~

After four days in the small restaurant located in Raton, New Mexico, Tabby wanted to be back in Topeka. The girls, while friendly enough, knew she was only temporary and often stayed to themselves. Loneliness assailed her on a daily basis.

She forced yet another smile and poured coffee for a man too engrossed in his newspaper to bother looking up to thank her. When she finished with him, she moved to the next and then the next, until she thought she'd scream.

A glance out the front window showed a dust storm thick enough to obscure visibility. There'd be no walk after work if a storm followed, and the early evening stroll was the one bright spot in Tabby's day.

She missed Adam and so wanted to tell him so. Close to tears, she shoved into the kitchen for fresh coffee.

"Good morning, Miss McClelland." Mr. Sullivan, the chef, wore his ever present grin. Orange hair peeked from beneath his tall hat.

"You're mighty chipper this morning, chef." Tabby grabbed the handles of a cart on which sat full carafes of freshly brewed coffee.

"I am." He waved a sheet of paper. "Didn't you tell me that you came from the Harvey House in Topeka?"

Her heart gave a stutter and she grabbed for the paper. "What happened? Is someone ill?"

"Of course not, silly girl. Why would they tell me if that was the case? It's my new assignment."

Of course it wouldn't be bad news. If it were, the man wouldn't be grinning. Wait. His new assignment could only mean..."Will the restaurant have two chefs?"

Please say yes. She couldn't bear it otherwise. What if Adam left before she returned? Why did it matter? Oh, she wanted to run away.

"Nope, the present head chef is headed to California. They've already got my replacement, and he arrives in a couple of days. Day after that, I'm headed to Kansas." The chef folded his letter and stuck it in the pocket of his apron. "Been waiting on an opportunity like this for a long time."

Mere days were left before Tabby would no longer be able to see Adam, talk with him about her day, admire the way his muscles rippled when he hefted large pots, see the understanding and compassion in his eyes after a particularly rough day of work. She had no swallow large enough to dislodge the lump in her throat. No words of comfort could heal her heart. She wrapped her arms around her middle and bent at the waist.

"Are you all right, Miss?" The chef looked into her eyes. "Want me to send someone for the wagon boss?"

"No. I just need some air."

"Go on, then. I'll have one of the kitchen gals deliver the coffee." He clapped and waved a hand.

"Thank you." Tabby straightened then dashed outside. She hefted her skirts and ran to the end of the street, disregarding the curious stares of bystanders. Chest heaving, tears streaming, she leaned against the wall of the livery.

Adam would be leaving soon. If not before she returned to Kansas, then shortly after. Confusion clouded her mind. She wanted to hop the next train back to him, but fear seized her heart in a fist of ice. Her heart told her Adam was a good man, a Godly man, but her mind told her that he could be like so many other men.

She was caught in a whirlpool of indecision and couldn't locate a lifeline. Wiping her tears on her apron, she headed back to work. A few days remained for her to find a solution to the dilemma in front of her. God willing, she'd find it before it was too late.

"Feeling better, Miss?" Chef Sullivan cast an anxious glance her way as she entered the kitchen. "I told the wagon boss you were indisposed. She wasn't pleased, but they covered for you."

"Thank you." Smoothing her hands down her dress, then poking her hair pins back in, Tabby prepared herself to return to work. She couldn't do anything about her feelings for Adam until she returned to Kansas, so she might as well do a good job in New Mexico.

After all, she heard rumors she might become a head waitress herself within the year. She had a difficult and important decision to make, and today was not the day to make it. She needed a clear mind and stable emotions.

She forced her mind to still as she went through motions as routine and common as sleeping. Smile, pour drinks, move to the next table. She had a stable job with a good income. A girl could ask for little else. Maybe if she told herself those words often enough she would actually believe them.

She splashed coffee onto one of the white tablecloths and scrubbed as hard as she could to prevent the liquid from staining. *Pay attention, Tabitha.*

She caught the eye of the head waitress, and mouthed an apology. As the day wore on, she barely held the tears at bay. By night time, she trembled from emotional exhaustion. Her nerves twanged so loudly she couldn't concentrate on her nightly prayers, except to say "Help me, God."

Which she whispered over and over into her pillow.

20

Adam froze as Tabby crossed the street. Now that he'd made up his mind to propose, he found his tongue as tied as the bow on the box he carried.

The hem of her royal blue skirt blew in the autumn wind. The breeze teased at strands of hair fallen free of her hat. She made the prettiest picture he'd ever seen.

He almost dropped the box of chocolates he'd purchased. He wanted to give her something when he told her of his feelings, and there were no flowers left from summer. The ring he someday intended to give to his bride was safe in his mother's hands. If he bought a woman other than his wife an article of clothing, his mother would arrive on the next train to kick his behind. Candy should be safe enough, and he knew Tabby enjoyed chocolate.

A large gust almost blew her hat from her head, and she reached up to hold it in place. With the other hand clutching her reticule, she increased her pace until she disappeared into the restaurant.

The urge to dash after her left him breathless. Soon, he'd tell her of his love and about Marilyn. Surely, she already knew about his feelings and would accept his offer of marriage.

His steps faltered. His heart skipped a beat. She could very possibly say no. Maybe all the signs he'd given her were only in his imagination. His palms sweated, leaving smudges on the candy box.

Images of Marilyn on her deathbed, face pale and drawn, filled his mind. He shook away the thoughts. He could keep Tabby safe in California. She was small but had already proven hardier than Marilyn whose frail beauty had been no match for farm life.

Again, he reminded himself that Tabby's life belonged to God. He could only do his best with the gifts given to him. He entered the restaurant and searched the main dining room. When he didn't see her there, he headed to the kitchen.

Tabby stood in the corner, folding tablecloths. He grinned. The woman couldn't be still for a moment. With her having arrived only moments before, he thought for sure she might relax a little. Possibly somewhere quiet where they could converse in private.

"Welcome back." The box dented where he clutched it. He relaxed his grip. "May I speak with you outside for a moment?"

"Certainly." She set the starched coverings on the counter and brushed past him, leaving the fresh scent of rose toilet water in her wake. Her manner was a bit cool, not that he blamed her after all. He hadn't had the nerve to see her off at the station. Instead, he'd hidden like a small boy from a scolding.

Nerves already on edge, they twanged now with the brush of her skirts against his leg. Once outside, he took a deep breath and thrust the candy at her. "I bought these for you."

She accepted the gift. "Thank you." Her eyes widened. "Did you sit on it? The box is crushed."

His neck heated. "No, just a too tight grip." He rubbed the back of his head where it met his neck, trying in vain to release the tension. "I'm sorry, Tabby, for not being at the station the other day, but…"

"It's no problem." She averted her gaze. "Please don't concern yourself."

"But it is." He laid a hand on top of hers.

She clamped her lips and stepped back. "We've gone over this, Adam, until I can't breathe with it."

"I was hoping you'd…"

"Chef." One of the kitchen helpers called through the open window. "I think something's burning. Well, maybe not burning, but rather boiling over."

"Well, take it off the stove." Must he do everything? He turned back to Tabby. "I need…"

"It's the soup for lunch, and it's running onto the floor."

"Go," Tabby said. "You're needed. Thank you very much for the chocolates. I will enjoy every piece." Her eyes softened. "We'll talk later, I promise."

"Uh." Hopefully, the note nestled inside the box would work on her heart until they could talk uninterrupted.

He barged into the kitchen where golden chicken broth spilled over a pan and onto the floor. "Did no one notice before it reached this point?" He refused to become one of those temperamental chefs clichés were made of, but when a man had intentions to propose to a beautiful woman, he did *not* want to be disturbed with kitchen disasters.

With a snap of his fingers, two busboys grabbed rags and knelt to wipe up the mess. Adam turned down the heat on the stove, donned his apron, and prepared his mind to focus on the task at hand. "We need more broth to replace what boiled over. Someone check the bread so it doesn't burn. We don't need to add another fiasco to the morning."

Some days he wondered why he bothered with help at all.

~

Tabby set the candy behind the lunch counter. If not for the timely interruption, she feared what Adam wanted to say to her, and how she would have to break his heart again. She hadn't made her decision yet, about whether to renew her contract or not. Did she want to be one of those girls who threw away the promise of independence and placed her trust in a man? Could she?

She covered her face with her hands. Why was the decision so hard? Either she wanted Adam or she didn't. Her flip-flopping wasn't fair to either of them. Oh, why couldn't a woman have both? A family and a career? Something other than a husband to give her value? Three cowboys sauntered into the restaurant, pulling her thoughts away from Adam. They plunked down at a table assigned to her and carried on a loud conversation, colored by cursing, with each other.

The manager, Mr. Richardson rushed to their table. "Please, gentlemen, lower your voices. There are children present."

One of the men, a tall bulky man with a dark beard, leaned his chair back on two legs. "Looks like they might be addin' to their vocabulary before we're gone. How long does it take to get any grub around here? We wanted to eat over at the saloon but their cook is out sick."

Tabby wished they'd stayed away. She grabbed some menus, took a deep breath, and marched in their direction. "Welcome to Harvey's. How may I serve you?"

"Hey, pretty thang!" Dark Beard grabbed her around the waist and tried to pull her onto his lap.

"This is not that type of establishment." She elbowed him in the nose, wincing at the sound of a crunch, and yanked free. Why didn't Mr. Richardson refuse them service? Surely, he didn't expect her to take these ruffians' orders.

The man laughed and grabbed for a napkin to stop his nose from bleeding down his shirtfront. "A real fiery filly. We might have to come here more often, boys. The scenery is a bit more classy than our usual haunt."

"I think not." Tabby tossed the menus on the table and whirled to leave.

Dark Beard grabbed her apron ties and tugged. "Eat with us. The saloon gals do."

"Leave her be or answer to me." Adam stood with fists clenched and a muscle ticking in his jaw. His narrowed eyes and dark tone showed he meant business.

Grateful for the diversion he caused, Tabby tore from the man's grasp and dashed around the counter.

One family stood from their table and hurried from

the restaurant without waiting for their food. Another man placed himself in front of the woman with him.

"You talking to me, fancy boy?" Dark Beard shoved Adam into a nearby table, sending plates of salad crashing to the floor.

Someone screamed.

One of Dark Beard's buddies pulled a gun from his waistband.

Adam came up swinging, and connected a right hook to Dark Beard's jaw. The man cursed and wrapped his arms around Adam's middle taking him to the floor in a huddle of cursing, flying fists, and flailing legs.

The gunman stepped around the table and headed toward the brawling men. Tabby clapped a hand over her mouth to cover her gasp. Adam was in trouble, with no one to come to his aid.

She grabbed the pistol under the lunch counter and circled the room. She needed to be where the customers would not be in the line of fire should she need to pull the trigger. Oh, she hoped things wouldn't come to that. She wasn't a very good shot.

"Stop right there." She planted her feet shoulder width apart and aimed the gun at the gunman. "I'm warning you."

The men continued to fight. The man with the weapon inched closer, his hand raised to land a blow to Adam's head. "Stop, cook boy, or I'll knock you across the room. I said stop." He fired into the ceiling, raining plaster.

A child cried, and people crowded the front doors.

"Please!" Mr. Richardson raised his hands. "This is not the place for this. Mr. Foster, I insist you get up."

The gunman whacked the restaurant manager behind

the ear. He collapsed to his knees, then scrambled for cover under a table.

Tabby's hand shook. She needed to stop the craziness before someone was seriously injured. She could shoot, but not very well. She needed to aim to the left of…She pulled the trigger and staggered back, blasting a hole in the lunch counter.

Time froze.

Adam shoved his assailant off of him. Black Beard lost the battle to keep his shirt blood free, and the stunned gunman turned to face Tabby. She lifted her chin and aimed the gun in a more direct line to a spot on his stained vest.

"Hey, little lady, I wasn't really going to shoot anyone."

"That's a sure thing now." She fought to keep her hands from shaking. "Drop the gun and kick it toward me."

Adam moved to her side. "Let me have that." He pried her fingers off the weapon, the corner of his mouth twitching. With the back of his other hand, he wiped blood from his lip.

Later, she'd find out what he considered so funny. In the meantime, she was too busy trying not to vomit. She moved behind the counter and slid to the floor. Light shined through the bullet hole in the wood counter. Miraculously, none of the lunch girls were injured by flying splinters. Tabby couldn't say the same for Adam's gift.

It lay in blasted bits of chocolate and white cardboard. The pretty blue ribbon dangled from a shelf like a forgotten ornament. Tabby's emotions lay as shattered as the candy.

Adam could have died that day, and she still didn't have the courage to tell him she loved him. She loved him!

She was a fool.

Tabby folded her arms on her knees, laid her forehead on her arms, and sobbed.

21

Adam knelt amongst the shattered dishes and chocolate and pulled Tabby's hands from her face. "Darling, are you hurt?"

"No." She sniffed and looked up. "But you are." She grabbed a napkin and dabbed at his lip. "I thought those men were going to kill you." She lowered her voice to a whisper. "Are they gone?"

"Carted off by the sheriff." Adam sat back. "You sure were something to see, standing up to those two ruffians. I'm not sure you needed me."

"My legs are trembling so bad, I don't think I can stand."

He chuckled. "Then don't. Sit here with me and relax a moment."

She narrowed her eyes. "You look amused again. What was so funny when I fired the gun?"

"The look on the men's faces. For them to be stood

up to by a little bit of a woman most likely damaged their egos beyond repair." And almost gave Adam a heart attack in the process. When he'd seen Tabby being manhandled, then standing up to the men, he thought he'd die.

Despite his worry, he wanted to ask whether she'd read the note inside the box where he expressed his undying love and asked her to be his wife. As skittish as she was about the subject, and after the way she skirted around the issue every time he hinted at marriage, he thought maybe a note would allow her time to think about what she wanted before she answered. He doubted either one of them could find the note in the wreckage from her misplaced shot.

Maybe he should ask her anyway. Spill his guts and profess his love. Yet something held him back. A voice told him to wait.

Tears still streamed down Tabby's face. Adam cupped her face and thumbed away the tears. "What's wrong? The danger is over. I'm here, safe and sound."

"I feel as if my dreams are as shattered as the dishes around me, as crushed as the candy I'm sitting in, and there's no one I can discuss them with."

"Me." A fist gripped his heart. "Why can't you talk to me?"

She shook her head. "You're the cause, Adam, don't you understand?" She pulled free and pushed to her feet. "You're at the root of all the emotions coursing through me."

He tugged her back to her knees. "Please." He pulled her close, claiming her lips, taking what he feared he'd never get again: A moment of love, of sweetness, of passion. "Come with me to California. Marry me. I leave in the morning."

"I can't." She sobbed. "I'm sorry." With one last tear-filled gaze, she straightened and dashed for the door.

Adam's heart lay in as many pieces as the crockery. What held her back? Surely she saw him as an honorable man by now. She certainly knew he loved her, didn't she? He slid against the wall, his legs splayed in front of him.

There'd been no heartache or heavy pursuing with Marilyn. Growing up together, they knew for years they would wed. After her death, Adam didn't think another woman could claim his heart. Now, he'd lost his heart to a woman who didn't want his love. He wanted to sob as hard as Tabby had.

Instead, he got to his feet with the speed of a tortoise. He had packing to do, and his family would arrive in the morning to pick him up. How disappointed Ma would be when a future bride didn't grace his arm when he greeted them.

He needed to let Tabby go.

~

Tabby patted some color into her cheeks and frowned at the dark circles under her eyes. Lack of sleep the night before had left her cranky and dry eyed. Knowing Adam was on his way out of Topeka, out of her life, left her feeling as if life had no meaning. She could very well be the loneliest woman on the planet. She shrugged at her dramatics and grabbed her reticule.

After the fiasco in the restaurant the day before, Miss O'Connor gave Tabby the day off to recover, and she planned to go shopping. One of the girls told her the mercantile got in a new shipment of women's apparel, and Tabby hoped shopping for a new pair of boots and a readymade dress would bolster her spirits. She'd made her choice to give up Adam, now she had to live with the decision despite the pain.

She ran her fingers over her lips, feeling his kiss. What would happen if she ran after him? Threw away everything she'd worked for and planned? Would that really be so awful? Did Adam really want a woman such as her by his side while he opened his own restaurant?

Absolutely not. He had no idea what he asked of her. She stilled. He'd asked her to marry him. She'd assumed it before from his kiss. She'd told him no and ran like a frightened rabbit. The final look he'd cast on her left her heart bleeding and broken. His love had shown through and pierced her.

But Adam had a family, loving parents. He'd see through her insecurities living and working side-by-side and wish he'd never wed her. He spoke of his first wife with pride. Tabby didn't know how to be a wife, a sister, a daughter-in-law.

She fell back onto the bed. All she knew how to be was a lonely child. Fresh tears welled. She thought she'd cried them all out the night before as she lay staring into the darkness of her room.

Approaching footsteps caused her to wipe her eyes and bolt from the bed. She marched from the room, down the stairs, and into sunshine that belied the shadow in her heart.

Her boot heels pounded the sidewalk as she hurried toward the mercantile. A box of chocolates, with a blue ribbon, might improve her mood. She'd gaze upon it and remember the moment Adam put one like it in her hands, and she'd dream of telling him yes instead of no.

What flavor of creams had he chosen? She wouldn't be able to duplicate it exactly without knowing. Had he purchased chocolates and vanilla or an assortment? She sagged against a wrought iron bench. A new box wouldn't be the same no matter how hard she tried to make it look identical.

Plastering a smile on her face, she shook off her melancholy mood and pushed through the mercantile doors. A young lady with light-colored hair, and an older woman who looked every bit like the girl's mother, glanced over their shoulders and smiled a greeting before turning back to the counter. The two waited while the shopkeeper wrapped their packages in brown paper.

Tabby nodded and headed for the shoes. She'd purchase some sort of candy when the counter cleared. Maybe a peppermint stick or lemon drop. Those were as far from chocolates as possible.

A pair of white lace up boots with a one inch heel screamed her name. She grabbed them to her chest and almost squealed in delight until she recognized their impracticalness. The boots were clearly meant for a bride or a nonworking lady. Something she might never be. She set them back on the shelf and moved to the black pairs.

"Those white ones are beautiful, aren't they?" Tabby turned to see the woman from the counter standing beside her.

"Yes, they are, but not practical for a Harvey Girl."

"How do you enjoy that profession?" The woman cocked her head to the side as if she were truly interested in Tabby's answer.

"I enjoy my job very much." She braced herself for ridicule.

"I'm Mary, dear. What's your name?"

Something about the woman invited friendship, confidence. So did the welcoming grin of the younger woman. Together, they put Tabby at ease. "I'm Tabitha McClelland."

Mary's eyes widened. "Oh. Well, it's nice to meet you. I can't help but notice the sad look in your eyes. Is there something I can do to help? We're leaving soon, but there's always time to pray."

"Most likely no one can help me." Why would a complete stranger want to help her? Why did Tabby find herself answering the personal questions? Maybe that was the draw. She could speak freely to a woman she would never see again.

"I had a choice to make—between love and a career." Tabby reached toward the spools of lace and twisted a strand of ivory around her fingers. "I'm not sure I made the right decision. Not that there is anything I could do anyway. I'm under contract for another month, and my work ethic won't allow me to quit before then. I'm afraid it's too late to even contemplate another decision."

"It's never too late." Mary patted her hand. "Do you care for this young man?"

"Very much."

"What does God tell you? Have you asked His will for your life?"

Tabby froze. "No."

Not once had she stopped and asked what God wanted her to do. She had needed a job, so she found one. Her life was horrible, so she started a new one. Not once did she stop and ask whether God had sent Adam to her. "I should probably do that right away."

"Most definitely." Mary shoved the boots into her hands. "And buy the boots, even if they are white. If a girl's got extra money, she can't ever go wrong with a pair of nice boots. And that light blue dress in the window would look absolutely beautiful on you. Life is too short. Treat yourself and enjoy." She turned to the younger woman. "Come along, Daphne. Your pa is waiting." Mary and her daughter sailed out the front door.

Daphne? The same Daphne that sent Adam a telegram saying his mother was ill? It couldn't be. Tabby's knees weakened. Had she spoken with Adam's mother just moments before? That meant he was still in town. Her heart leaped.

Dropping the boots, Tabby lifted her skirts and dashed into the street. The women were nowhere to be found. Neither was Adam. Oh, Lord, which way could they have gone? Tears stung her eyes. She'd missed her chance again to tell Adam of her true feelings.

The white steeple of the church rose in the distance. Seek God's will? She'd do it now. She'd storm heaven's gate for an answer. Yet, somewhere in her heart, she felt she already knew what God would tell her.

The church sanctuary welcomed her with a quiet peace. Tabby made her way to the front row, sat on the polished pew, and then fixed her gaze on the simple wood cross on the wall.

"What would you have me do, God?" She folded her hands in her lap. "I love Adam. I will admit that now, and it may be too late. Am I so broken that I'm unable to accept love from a man?" She uttered the last words with a sob, forcing them through a clogged throat.

The light through the window cast a lilac shadow on the wall by the time Tabby stood. Filled with peace, she knew the path she would take. She blew a kiss at the cross and almost skipped out the door.

It might be a month before she could act on her decision, but if she worked hard, time would fly. And first thing in the morning, she'd head to the mercantile to buy the white boots and blue dress.

22

Tabby dragged her suitcase out of the restaurant and onto the sidewalk. Jobless again, yet this time her heart leaped in anticipation of what lay down the road. In her hand, she clutched a first class ticket to San Francisco, California. Harvey contract fulfilled, she was now free to act on what she truly believed to be God's will for her. Hopefully, it wasn't too late, and Adam would be overjoyed to see her.

Within minutes, two of the restaurant's kitchen staff came outside and toted her trunk and bag to the train depot. Miss O'Connor stood at the door and waved a white handkerchief, her eyes red with tears. Tabby returned her wave, pleased the woman swore she'd find no one of Tabby's caliber to replace her.

Well, if things didn't work out in San Francisco, Tabby might very well have to return to Topeka. She carried an unsigned contract in her bag, just in case

Adam dejected her and she needed to console herself with work. She prayed not. Every night since her lonely vigil in church she'd shed tears over letting him get away. Only what she perceived as God's promise kept her going until her contract was up.

Now, the sun warmed her face despite a brisk fall breeze, a blue sky overhead promised a bright future, and the whistle of the arriving train announced a glorious adventure ahead. In Tabby's bag were the white boots and blue dress, what she hoped would be her wedding clothes.

The train whooshed to a stop, blowing Tabby's skirts. She'd come full circle. Six months ago, she'd stood on another platform and waited for a train that would lead her to the next chapter of her life. Now, another, better one waited. One where Tabby would embrace love offered and not shove it away in fear.

God had opened her heart, her mind, and her future with endless possibilities.

"All aboard!" The conductor cupped his mouth, then held down a hand to assist Tabby in boarding. "Enjoy your trip, ma'am."

"Thank you." Sweeping aside her new blue and white striped traveling costume, she made her way to her first class seat. This time the pleasure of being waited on hand and foot, having a nice bunk to sleep in, none of it would come as a surprise, but rather a blessing from God who looked out for all her needs. Even the ones she herself was unaware of.

The journey into God's loving arms had been a long, hard one, but she'd made it. She couldn't wait to tell Adam the news.

The train chugged from the station. Tabby clasped

her hands in her lap. Her leg jerked up and down like a butter churn. How would she ever survive the journey? Oh, she wished she could fly.

She stilled. What if Adam rejected her? It'd been over thirty days since he left. She'd wounded him dreadfully. Most likely, he carried that hurt deep inside and would spurn her. She clutched the lace at her throat. She had to at least try.

"Coffee or tea?" The server, wearing a uniform very similar to the ones left hanging in Tabby's former room, wheeled a silver cart with a tea pot and cups.

"Tea, please." Tabby waited to be served then turned back to the window. Why must the train move so slowly?

She leaned her forehead against the cool glass of the window and remembered the first train ride when Adam came to her rescue against another man's unwelcome advances. He'd pretended to be her husband. How she wished, now, that he were.

At dinner, Tabby picked at her roast chicken and potatoes. Her mind whirled with the thought that Adam might no longer want her. She had no one to blame but herself. Surely, California had a multitude of jobs for a hardworking girl. She sipped her lukewarm coffee. But she no longer wanted a career, unless it was helping Adam in his restaurant.

The train jerked, brakes screeching, and came to a stop. Coffee splashed onto Tabby's new clean shirtwaist. She grabbed her napkin and dabbed at the stain.

Men ran down the aisle and shouts rang through the open windows at the front of the car. Spilled coffee forgotten, Tabby knelt on the seat and lowered her window to peer out. Men milled around the track. Were they being robbed? She fiddled with the lace at her throat. She'd heard nightmarish tales of train robbers. There'd be little sleep that night.

After what seemed an hour, but was more likely thirty minutes with no news, she made her way through the car and to the metal deck outside. A curse reached her ears followed by the whack of an ax. The moon played hide-n-seek, making the commotion at the front of the train impossible to make out.

Having heard no gunshots, she determined it wasn't a robbery. How she wanted to go see what had happened. Surely, if the train jumped the track she would have felt more than a jerk.

Since there didn't seem to be any immediate danger, she headed down the stairs, thankful she'd dawdled over dinner instead of heading to her cabin. The long train ride didn't provide a lot of excitement.

"Please stay back, ma'am." The conductor tried to usher her back to the train.

"I have a desperate need to stretch my legs." Tabby craned her neck.

"You may do so in the cars."

"No, I don't think so, although I do appreciate your concern." What was going on in front of the train?

A shrill whistle drew the conductor's attention, and he jogged away.

It wasn't easy trying to walk with stealth on pebbles, but Tabby hitched her skirts and did her best. She stepped in front of the train and gasped at the sight of an overturned wagon. She whipped back and forth. Where were the people?

She grabbed the arm of a man in striped coveralls.

"Where is the wagon's driver? The horse?"

"We've cut the horse free, ma'am, and dragged him to the bushes. There was no driver."

"Praise God." Oh, the poor horse, apparently so frightened he'd bolted onto the tracks and in front of the train. At least no one else was injured or worse. "How long until we are on our way?"

"Not for several hours. You'd best head back to the train. We'll do our best to get moving, but there are steps to take. The wagon is in pieces for one thing. Might take a while to clear the pieces away."

Tabby's shoulders slumped. At this rate, it would take forever to reach San Francisco. Adam would definitely have forgotten about her.

~

Adam put the last coat of varnish on the restaurant's sign and stepped back to admire his handiwork. Foster's Eatery. Sure had a nice ring to it, in his opinion. They ought to be ready to open in a week. He sighed and set the stained rag next to its pail.

Maybe a day spent at the beach would lift his morale, clear his thoughts. Anything to get Tabby out of his head. Over a month, and she still occupied most of his thoughts. When would his love for her fade, the ache in his heart lessen?

"Stop being so melancholy," Ma told him. She dried her weathered hands on a faded apron. "I told you she would come, and we have too much work to do for you to stare off into the wild blue yonder."

He sighed. "It's been over a month. Her contract expired a week ago." Using a hammer, he pounded the lid onto the metal can of varnish. "She chose her job over me."

Ma reached up and smacked the back of his head. "Are you calling me a liar? I said she would come, and she will. I told you what she said in the mercantile. That woman is as smitten as you are, although I'm thinking she might be a bit smarter."

"You were nicer when you were sick." Adam laughed and popped her with the rag.

"I love you, son." Ma cupped his cheek. "Be patient. God has a new wife for you, and I believe Tabitha is the one. You are a lucky man to have two such loves in your lifetime."

Adam kissed her cheek. "No, Pa is the lucky one. He's had his whole life with just you."

Her cheeks pinked. "Tabitha loves you. She said so herself, and she is as far from Marilyn as possible. Which, of course, is a good thing, so you can't compare the two. You were married such a short time. You have many, many years ahead of you."

"How did you get so wise?" He forced the question past a tortured throat. Comparison wasn't a thing he'd considered, but his mother made a good point. At the age of twenty-five, he and Tabby had many years ahead of them. If she showed up.

"A lot of living." Ma gave his face another pat, then headed into the store room at the back of the restaurant.

Adam smiled and shook his head. She was completely convinced that Tabby would show up on their doorstep some day and profess her love. Well, he'd given up on the idea. It was time to move forward, and that meant getting the restaurant up and running. Which wouldn't happen if he continued standing around daydreaming.

"Afternoon, son." Pa carried in a bag of wheat and

propped it in the corner. "Got a wagon load of supplies if you've got a minute." Already the worry of the farm had lessened from his shoulders and the lines on his face were less pronounced. Adam thanked God every day for the opportunity to own the restaurant and live with fresh ocean breezes.

"I'm ahead of schedule." Adam stashed the pail behind the counter that would serve as a lunch bar in a few days. "I've more than a few minutes to spare."

"Daphne's working on some posters to hire help. Ought to have them complete by morning. That red paint you wanted for the front door came in today," Pa said handing a bucket to Adam. "Don't know why you want a red door, but it's fine with me."

"I want to be able to make the place easy to find." They could tell potential customers they were the red door on Market Street.

They worked until night fall and the light faded too much for them to see. After promising his family he'd be home soon, Adam perched on the top step of the restaurant's recently built back stoop, his arm around Twister. The dog was a poor substitute for Tabby.

Why had he built something he knew would hurt him? Rubbing his hand over the wood, he winced as a splinter sunk itself into his finger. Building the stoop made him feel closer to Tabby. He could see the look on her face when he showed it to her.

She'd remember the conversations and closeness they'd shared. He treasured even the precious moments when they barely spoke a word.

Clouds dissipated, allowing the moon to shine a path across the lawn. What he wouldn't give to see Tabby run along that silver path and throw herself into his arms. He was a poetic fool, waiting for someone who most likely chose to stay away. Tabby seemed too afraid to trust anyone. But, he'd prayed that she could learn to trust him.

He'd laid his heart before her and God. He'd given her over to his Lord. Yet, here he sat, feeling like an old man whose life was on a downward slope. If Ma could read his thoughts, she'd try taking a switch to his behind, no matter his age.

Chuckling, he picked up a stick and drew squiggles in the dirt. A train whistle blew off in the distance. Such a mournful sound. For two days last week, he'd actually been dumb enough to stand on the train platform to surprise Tabby when she got off.

Maybe Ma heard her wrong, that day at the mercantile. Daphne hadn't heard Tabby say she loved him, but she said she'd been engrossed in some pearl buttons. He groaned and tossed the stick for Twister to fetch.

He stiffened. He'd drawn a heart in the dirt with "Adam loves Tabby" written inside.

He should have drawn it as a broken heart.

23

Tabby stuffed her nightgown into her bag. Next stop, San Francisco. Her heart threatened to burst through her corset and layers of cotton. What if she'd made the long trip in vain? Having Adam reject her after all this time made more sense than him welcoming her with open arms. *God, please, let him still love me.*

The train lurched. She lost her footing, slammed her hip into the wall, and dropped her bag. Wonderful. She could limp her way through San Francisco. She knelt to retrieve the bag. The train came to a stop. Her head did the same, against the steel foundation of her bunk. She prayed the rest of her time in California wouldn't be as painful.

With a deep breath, she straightened, luggage in hand, and made her way to the platform to wait for her trunk. She'd have to wait until she could store it, when all she wanted was to search for Adam. She stood, foot tapping, and watched as families reunited with loved ones.

Maybe she should have taken the chance on a telegram. Then Adam could have met her, or not. But she would have known then, the moment she stepped from the train, instead of still wondering about her reception.

She stepped aside as a man barreled past her and swept a woman into his arms. She sighed, blinked away tears, and moved into the train station office.

Approaching the ticket agent, she opened her reticule. "I need to store my trunk for a day or two."

The man peered at her over wire spectacles. "It'll cost you a dollar. Your name on the trunk?"

"Yes, sir."

"Write down your name and a description of the trunk. We'll hold onto it for three days. That's Wednesday, don't forget."

"I won't. Please watch it carefully. It contains my wedding clothes." Tabby peeled a dollar off the small roll of cash, filled out the required information, then handed him the paper and money. "Thank you. I'm looking for a restaurant."

"Lady, there's lots of them."

"Owned by a man named Adam Foster." *Please say you know him.*

"Sure, I know him. His place is on Market Street. Has a red door. You can't miss it." He looked over her shoulder at the next person in line. Tabby's cue to leave.

"Thank you." She rushed from the station and to a waiting buggy for hire. Getting to her destination as quickly as possible would make the use of precious funds worth the expense. She climbed into the buggy. "Market Street, please."

The driver, a wizened dark skinned man with hunched shoulders, nodded. "Any particular place?"

"Foster's?"

"Right away." He clicked to the horse, and then ambled away from the train.

Tabby settled back against the hard wood of the seat. Her breathing increased to the point she feared she'd pass out and fall under the horse's hooves. She made it. Within minutes, she'd look upon Adam's face.

What would she see? Regret? Dislike? Happiness? Her hands trembled in the folds of her skirt.

By the time the buggy stopped in front of a storefront which displayed a grand sign saying Foster's Eatery, she'd worked herself into quite a dither. She paid the man, and climbed from her seat without waiting for his assistance. She heard a rip as her skirt caught on something, but instead of slowing, she yanked the new traveling costume free and dashed for the bright red door.

Closed? Of course. Adam wouldn't have his business open on a Sunday. Her shoulders slumped.

A paper tacked beside the door caught her attention. Help Wanted. She snatched the page to her chest. She'd approach Adam about the job. Tomorrow. He would have to see her then.

In the meantime, she'd wander the streets in search of a place to spend the night. If restaurants abounded, so must hotels. Preferably one by the ocean. She'd always wanted to see the sea.

Refusing to let the setback deter her or stomp her spirit, she set off at a brisk pace in the direction she thought to be west. Ignoring the glances and occasional whistles due a woman traveling alone, she marched as fast as her skirts would allow until she faced the lapping shore.

A salt-filled breeze caressed her face. She breathed deep of the clean air, closed her eyes, and listened to one of the most beautiful sounds God ever created. Oh, why hadn't she made the trip before? All her complaining about wanting adventure, and she'd never before faced such a marvelous sight.

Her feet suddenly felt too confined in her shoes. She sat on the sand and removed them, even being so daring as to remove her stockings. Shoes and stockings in hand she raced to the water's edge. The water kissed her tired toes and washed away the stress of the day and the worries of tomorrow.

Pure heaven. She shaded her eyes with one hand and gazed across the silvery blue expanse kissed by diamonds scattered by the sun. What she wouldn't give to sit there on a cool evening with Adam's arms around her to keep her warm. The moon would replace the sun and provide a backdrop more romantic than anything she could imagine.

She turned and headed down the beach, keeping her feet on the cool sand, splashed by waves. What did it matter if her dress was ruined? She'd bought it with Adam in mind. It was already too mussed and stained to wear another day.

A few yards away, a man sat cross-legged in the sand, and leaned back on tanned arms. The wind mussed his dark blond hair. Singing drifted down the sand.

Tabby's heart stopped.

~

Adam closed his eyes, spending his morning in God's love, rejoicing in His promises. His family had yet to find a new church home so the beach gave him a place to worship with no one around but him and God.

He softly sang the lyrics to Amazing Grace, sending the words out to sea and up to heaven. The restaurant opened tomorrow, and he sang his praises to the One who let his dream come true. At least one of them. Well, he wouldn't complain. He'd known Tabby's feelings from the very beginning.

God held it all in His hands. Marilyn's death, selling the farm, the restaurant, and Tabby's choice for her life. While Adam's heart had healing to do, he'd made peace with her decision.

A wave came farther than before and soaked him. He shivered but didn't move. Ma was used to him coming home with salt-stiffened clothes.

"Red's my favorite color."

"Is it?" She came! Adam clenched his hands together and kept his gaze focused on the rolling waves.

Tabby lowered herself beside him and wrapped her arms around her knees. A sheet of paper fluttered from one hand. "I've come to apply for the job."

Adam fought to keep from grinning. "I'm afraid I'll have to interview you."

"I'm ready."

The words seeped into his heart, filling the empty space. "Proceed. Tell me about yourself."

She took a deep breath. "My name is Tabitha McClelland, and I'm a fool. I've been a lost child my entire life, and I'm looking for my home. Will you help me find it?"

He turned so fast he almost fell over. He grabbed her empty hand. "It's right here." He placed her hand over his heart. "It's always been right here. There's only one job I want for you. Will you accept it?"

"If it's the position as Mrs. Adam Foster, I'll accept it gladly." Her eyes shimmered with tears.

Wrapping his arms around her, he pulled her close, pulling them both to a standing position and tucking her head under his chin. "No more gladly than I offer. What took you so long to come? I'd almost given up hope."

"I had to fulfill my contract. I've never quit anything in my life, except for almost letting you get away." She shuddered. "I met the wisest woman in the mercantile the day you left who told me life was short and to buy the boots."

"Boots?" What in the world was she talking about?

"The most beautiful pair of white boots in the world. After she left, and I realized you'd left, I sat in church for hours and talked to God. I came to terms with my father, Adam. He was one man. One poor, misguided, ill and sinful man. And my mother was just as weak. I almost followed in her footsteps. We are nothing like them." Her arms snaked around his waist. "Will you kiss me?"

"Oh, sweetheart." He tilted her face to his and placed his lips on hers. He kissed her until she sagged against his chest, and his legs threatened to give way.

Relinquishing his hold on her precious lips, he pulled an arm's length away. "I'm tired of waiting. I want to marry you now. Tomorrow, at the latest. Will you come meet my family?" He motioned his head toward a white cottage on the horizon. "We've rented a house by the shore. Marry me here, in this spot."

"Oh, Adam." Her tears increased, turning into sobs. "How can you forgive me for my stupidity?"

"I can forgive you anything." He wiped away her tears. "Let's go."

"I look such a mess. My dress is ruined, my feet are bare, and my face must be red."

"You're beautiful." He kissed her again. "I think you'll be barefoot a lot while we're here. This is our new spot. No more back stoops."

She grinned and placed her hand in his. "Most definitely, Mr. Foster."

Hand in hand they made their way to the house where Ma already stood, hand shading her eyes, on the porch. He should have known she would notice the presence of a young woman on the beach. If the smile on her face was any indication, she also knew who the lady was.

"My dear." Ma dashed to greet them. "Did you buy the boots?"

Tabby nodded. "I plan to wear them tomorrow."

Ma cried and pulled her close, leaving Adam feeling suddenly alone. "Excuse me, but she will be my bride."

"And my second daughter." Ma slapped his arm. "You behave and go warn your Pa. We don't want him having a heart attack when you walk in with your news."

Adam shook his head, placed a kiss on the top of Ma's head, and pushed through the door. Tabby was in good hands. But only for a moment. He intended to steal her back in seconds and never let her go again. "Pa, I'm getting married."

"About time, son." Pa came from the parlor. "Overdue, I'd say." He clapped a hand on Adam's shoulder. "I assume it's with the wind tossed lovely on the porch with Ma?"

"That's the one. We're getting married on the beach tomorrow at this time."

Pa nodded. "I'll fetch a preacher. Don't worry. All you have to do is show up."

Adam had no intentions of doing anything else. He didn't know where Daphne had been hiding, but if her shriek was any indication, she'd joined the bevy of females on the back porch. Life couldn't be grander. Adam wanted to fall to his knees and thank God for his blessings. But that would have to wait. First, he wanted to kiss his bride-to-be some more and right now, the crowd was too large to suit him.

"Okay, Ma, Daphne," he called, joining the women. "Let me have her back. We've things to discuss. Go get your best dresses ready. There's a wedding tomorrow."

Ma cried louder, Daphne hugged Tabby, and Adam grabbed Tabby's hand. "Let's run while we can."

They dashed back across the sand, scattering shoes, stockings, and whatever else Tabby had kept in her hands. They stopped at the water's edge and Adam pulled her back into his arms.

They had a lot of kissing to make up for.

24

Tabby sat in a high-backed straight chair and stared at the white boots on the floor in front of her. Walking in the sand would be difficult in shoes with a heel no matter how modest. She smiled. No, she'd go barefoot and carry the boots. Just as she had done yesterday when finding her love on the beach.

"You look beautiful." Mrs. Foster dabbed at her eyes. "That's the dress from the mercantile window. Oh, and the…boots."

Tabby stood and hugged her future mother-in-law. "This is all your doing, Mrs. Foster. If you hadn't met me in the mercantile…"

"Pshaw." She waved a hand. "Please, call me Ma. We're family. I haven't seen Adam this happy in such a long time. It does this old heart good."

"I'll do everything in my power to make sure he stays that way."

"Just love him." Ma cupped her face. "And I can see that you do."

"With everything in me." Tears stung Tabby's eyes. God was so good to her, and all she'd done previously was feel sorry for the life she'd had as a child. A difficult life, but one that prepared her to know, and cherish, happiness when she found it.

"Will you miss your life as a Harvey Girl?" Ma tucked a piece of hair that had fallen loose from her bun back under its pin.

"No. I enjoyed that life, but this is the one God has called me to." Amazement over the revelation wouldn't dissipate anytime soon. For a girl who'd always yearned for a steady job and adventure, marriage offered more than she'd dreamed in both areas.

"Okay." Ma shook out the hem of Tabby's dress, then handed her a bouquet of daisies. "I'm going to the beach. You and Daphne come along when you can. I'm sure Adam is as jittery as a June bug." She gave Tabby a kiss then left the room.

No more so than Tabby. She lifted her trembling hands when Daphne entered the room. "I'll fall before I get there."

Daphne shook her head and took Tabby's hands. "I'll be with you the whole way. After all, Adam is waiting. I'm sure if you fall, he will break his fool neck rushing to your aid."

Tabby giggled, picturing the sight of her sitting in the sand in her new dress with Adam sprawled before her in his best clothes. "Yes, I guess he would." He'd storm hell's gates if she needed him to.

She peered out the window. The sun was beginning to set. She'd have to hurry to be there on time. Adam wanted the sky pink like her cheeks, he'd said. She flushed at his words, eager to become Mrs. Foster.

With a deep breath, she nodded. "Time to go." Her heart leaped.

~

"Don't turn around yet son, she's got a ways to walk, and you don't want to ruin the surprise," Pa said. "But your bride is as lovely as the flowers she carries."

Adam shook his arms to release the tension in his shoulders. This was it. The day he got married to the love of his life. He cast a glance heavenward. He'd loved Marilyn, no doubt about it, but knew deep in his soul that Tabby was the one God created as his other half. He knew it as sure as he knew he needed to breathe to live. "Tell me when she's close enough for me to see her face clearly."

"Oh." Ma fanned her hands in front of her face. "I'm going to be all red and puffy by the time she gets here."

Pa put his arm around her shoulders. "We don't want you to outshine the bride, now do we?"

"Stop." She hit his shoulder. "You can turn now, son. The ocean plays a beautiful wedding march, doesn't it?"

Adam nodded, glanced at a seagull soaring overhead, the stark white of his feathers in direct contrast with an azure sky. He took a deep breath before he turned.

A vision in blue picked her way across the sand, white boots in one hand, white daisies in the other. She'd come barefoot, just as she'd said she would. His grin almost split his face. While Daphne looked lovely in a dress of green, he couldn't take his eyes off Tabby.

He dug his toes into the sand. Most people might think it improper for them to get married without shoes, but not him. Not when this was the exact spot where she had agreed to be his wife.

Tabby's eyes glistened as Daphne took her bouquet, then went to stand with Ma and Pa. Tears stung Adam's eyes. *Thank you, God, for this wonderful gift.*

The pastor cleared his throat. "Dearly beloved, we are gathered…"

Adam wasn't sure what else was said, so engrossed was he on his bride's face. Their gazes locked. He hardly blinked. He must have said all the right things, made all the right gestures, because the next thing he heard was, "You may now kiss the bride."

With a squeal, Tabby threw herself into his arms. He grabbed her close, dipped her back, and planted one long kiss on her delicious lips while his family cheered. How he looked forward to doing so as often as he pleased.

"I love you, Mrs. Foster."

"And I love you, Mr. Foster."

~

DEAR READER

The Harvey Girls were an important part of American History, and I hope you enjoyed spending time with them as much I enjoyed writing their stories. While I read many personal accounts of the Harvey Girls, I took liberties with the people working in the restaurants, and the timeframes depicted. Unable to find any information on opening dates except for knowing that new Harvey restaurants were continually opening along the railroad, I also took the liberty of placing restaurants where needed and in the timeframes needed to move my story forward.

Harvey Girls were trained in Kansas, and as the railroad moved westward more restaurants opened along the line. The Harvey House in Raton, New Mexico, did not belong to Fred Harvey until 1882.

I have no idea if such persons as Mr. Hastings or Miss O'Connor existed. From the true accounts I've read, the Harvey restaurants were known for friendly, exemplary service and were a wonderful place of employment.

I wanted to portray people chasing their dreams, and since women were just beginning to be accepted into the workforce, I thought it timely to have Tabby struggle with the issue some of the historical Harvey Girls struggled with in the very beginning.

Some people in the beginning of the Harvey restaurants frowned upon the women being called to serve, and many women did find their husbands while working in the famous restaurants along the Santa Fe railroad. I hope I entertained you with a sweet love story and a fictional behind the scenes look at the Women Who Tamed the West.

Cynthia Hickey

Don't miss the other Harvey Girl stories:
>> Guiding With Love
>> Serving With Love
>> Warring With Love

ABOUT THE AUTHOR

Multi-published and Amazon Best-Selling author Cynthia Hickey had three cozy mysteries and two novellas published through Barbour Publishing. Her first mystery, Fudge-Laced Felonies, won first place in the inspirational category of the Great Expectations contest in 2007. Her third cozy, Chocolate-Covered Crime, received a four-star review from Romantic Times. All three cozies have been re-released as ebooks through the MacGregor Literary Agency, along with a new cozy series, all of which stay in the top 50 of Amazon's ebooks for their genre. She has several historical romances releasing in 2013, 2014, 2015 through Harlequin's Heartsong Presents, and has sold more than 300,000 copies of her works. She is active on FB, twitter, and Goodreads, and is a contributor to Cozy Mystery Magazone blog and Suspense Sisters blog. Her and her husband run the small press, Forget Me Not Romances, which includes some of the CBA's well-known authors. She lives in Arizona with her husband, one of their seven children, two dogs and two cats. She has five grandchildren who keep her busy and tell everyone they know that "Nana is a writer". Visit her website at www.cynthiahickey.com

CPSIA information can be obtained
at www.ICGtesting.com
Printed in the USA
LVHW04s1717090918
589613LV00003B/473/P

9 781512 262926